The Correspondence of Fradique Mendes
A Novel

THE CORRESPONDENCE
OF FRADIQUE MENDES
A NOVEL

José Maria de Eça de Queirós

Translated from the Portuguese
by Gregory Rabassa

TAGUS PRESS
UMass Dartmouth
Dartmouth, Massachusetts

Adamastor Series 6
Center for Portuguese Studies and Culture

General Editor: Frank F. Sousa
Editorial Manager: Gina Reis
Manuscript Editor: Anna M. Klobucka
Graphic Designer: Spencer Ladd

Editorial Board: João Cezar de Castro Rocha & Phillip Rothwell

This publication was made possible in part by a grant from the
Luso-American Foundation

For all inquiries, please contact:
Tagus Press at UMass Dartmouth
Center for Portuguese Studies and Culture
285 Old Westport Road
North Dartmouth MA 02747-2300
Tel. 508-999-8255
Fax 508-999-9272
www.portstudies.umassd.edu

Library of Congress Cataloging-in-Publication Data

Queirós, Eça de, 1845–1900.
[Correspondencia de Fradique Mendes. English]
The correspondence of Fradique Mendes / by J.M. de Eça de Queirós ; translated from the
Portuguese by Gregory Rabassa.
    p. cm. — (Adamastor book series ; 6)
ISBN 978-1-933227-32-0 (alk. paper)
1. Travelers—Portugal—Fiction. 2. Epistolary fiction. 3. Satire. I. Rabassa, Gregory. II. Title.
PQ9261.E3C613 2010
869.33—dc

Contents

Editor's Note

José Maria de Eça de Queirós *or* Queiroz (1845–1900) is Portugal's best known and most translated novelist of the nineteenth century. José Saramago called him "Portugal's greatest novelist" and Harold Bloom considers him "a writer of genius."

Eça de Queirós, as he is commonly known, was born in Póvoa do Varzim (north of Oporto) to a woman who later married his father, a magistrate. Eça would only live with his parents for fewer than five years, after completing his studies in law at Coimbra, and was only officially recognized as a legitimate son when he married at the age of forty-one. He was a diplomat as consul, first in Cuba (1872–74), then in England (1874–88), and finally in France, more specifically, Paris, from 1889 until his death in 1900.

His work is usually divided into three distinct phases: the Romantic, from the 1860s, consisting mostly of short stories (and essays) with a fantastic and gothic flair, often seen as influenced by Edgar Allen Poe and Baudelaire; the Realist-Naturalist period, spanning almost two decades and including novels of social satire in the tradition of Balzac, Flaubert, and Zola, to wit: *The Crime of Father Amaro* (1876, 1880), *Cousin Bazilio* (1878), and *The Maias* (1888). And the last phase, the so-called and still not clearly defined Later Eça, which includes two novels that coincide with the second phase—namely, *The Mandarin* (1880) and *The Relic* (1887), with fantastic voyages to China and the Holy Land, respectively—and three posthumous novels published within a year of the author's death: *The Illustrious House of Ramires, The Correspondence of Fradique Mendes*, and *The City and the Mountains*.

The Correspondence of Fradique Mendes, which Eça published in serial form in a newspaper in 1888 and then continued to revise until his death, is a fictional, comical biography of an esthete, anti-bourgeois dandy, and man-about-the-world reminiscent of an Oscar Wilde or a Pessoa heteronym. The novel comprises a novella—to use the author's own term—written by a fictional, naive and, therefore, ironic admirer who introduces the letters. These are addressed to real people—literary and intellectual friends of the author Eça de Queirós—and to fictional characters. Curiously, Fradique Mendes is a poet originally conceived in 1869–70 by Eça and two friends who published, in a Portuguese newspaper and as a joke on their fellow countrymen, satanic poems à la Baudelaire under the pseudonym of Carlos Fradique Mendes. But Eça alone develops the earlier imagined poet, obsessed with form, into a full-fledged protagonist in a novel.

Eça's later works, including *The Correspondence of Fradique Mendes,* have maintained their freshness and relevance to today's reader. The extraordinary style in which they are written, and the issues they raise—from the relationship between language (fiction) and reality, between the past and its recovery in the present through historiography, between technology and the human, and between the latter and the environment—are still of importance and more pertinent than ever.

The Correspondence of Fradique Mendes is here masterfully rendered into English for the first time by Gregory Rabassa, the translator of several Nobel laureates from Latin America (including Gabriel García Márquez and Mario Vargas Llosa), the nineteenth-century Brazilian novelist Machado de Assis (Eça's great rival in the Portuguese language), and contemporary Portuguese authors such as António Lobo Antunes.

—Frank F. Sousa

The Correspondence of Fradique Mendes
A Novel

Fradique Mendes
(Remembrances and Notes)

I

My close friendship with Fradique Mendes had its start in Paris in 1880 at East-ertime, precisely during the week he had just returned from southern Africa. My acquaintance with this admirable man, however, dates back to Lisbon in the distant year 1867. It was in the summer of that year, one afternoon at the Café Martinho, when in a dog-eared copy of the *Revolução de Setembro* I came across the name C. Fradique Mendes in huge letters beneath some poetry that made me marvel.

The themes ("emotional motifs," as we called them in 1867) of those five or six poems, printed together under the title *Inscriptions*, immediately caught me with their captivating and welcome originality. It was during the time when my companions in the Cenacle and I, dazzled by the epic lyricism of the *Légende des siècles*, "the book that a great wind has carried down to us from Guernsey," went about abominating and combating with stern outcries the intimate lyri-cism, cloistered in two inches of the heart and understanding nothing among all the sounds of the universe except the swish of Elvira's skirts, which was turn-ing poetry, especially in Portugal, into a monotonous, endless tale of love's glo-ries and martyrdoms.[1] Fradique Mendes, then, was evidently one of those young poets who, following the peerless Master of the *Légende des siècles*, were heading off in universal sympathy in search of emotional motifs beyond the heart's lim-ited beating: to history, legend, custom, and religion, everything that down through the ages in diverse and unique ways has defined and revealed mankind. And at the same time Fradique Mendes was working a vein of poetry that drew me in: modernity, the delicate and sober notation of the delights and horrors of life, the life we have around us, which we can bear witness to or sense along the streets we all tramp, in the houses next door to ours, in the humble destinies that slip along by us in the humble shadows.

Those little poems of the *Inscriptions* were truly a magnificent revelation of new themes. There an allegorical saint, a sixth-century hermit, was dying in the snows of Silesia, attacked and dominated by such an unexpected and bestial rebellion of the flesh, when he was right on the brink of blessedness, that he was suddenly losing his holiness, and with it the divine and costly fruit of fifty years of penitence and hermitage. A crow, eloquent and old beyond all age, was telling of the time he had been part of a merry flock that followed Caesar's legions through all the Gauls, and then Alaric's hordes as they rolled on toward Italy, all in white marble against a blue background. The good knight Percival, mirror and flower of idealists, was leaving behind, through city and countryside, the silent furrow of his golden armor, passing through the whole world over long epochs of time in search of the Holy Grail, that mystical cup filled with the blood of Christ, which he had seen pass by glimmering among the clouds, above the towers of Camerlon. A Satan of Germanic invention, well read in Spinoza and Leibniz, was singing in the alleyways of a medieval city an ironic serenade to the stars, "drops of light frozen in the cold air" . . . And among these motifs of splendid symbolism came the picture of simple modernity, the "Little Old Ladies," five small old women with gaily printed shawls over their shoulders, a kerchief or a basket in hand, sitting on a stone bench in a long and longing silence, illuminated by the remains of the autumn sun.

I can't vouch, however, for the accuracy of these charming bits of reminiscence. After that August afternoon in the Martinho, I couldn't find any more *Inscriptions* or what there was in them that had caught my attention at the time. It wasn't the idea but rather the form, a superb form of plasticity and life that reminded me, at the same time, of the sculptured marble verses of Leconte de Lisle, but with a warmer blood coursing through their chiseled veins, and of Baudelaire's intense nervous energy vibrating with greater form and cadence. It was precisely that year, 1867, that J. Teixeira de Azevedo and I, along with some other comrades, had discovered in the heaven of French poetry (the only one to which our eyes were lifted) a whole pleiad of new stars where, standing out for their superior and special brightness, were these two suns—Baudelaire and Leconte de Lisle. Victor Hugo, whom at that time we used to call "Papa Hugo" or "The Almighty Hugo," wasn't a star for us but was God Himself, first and forever, from whom the stars received their light, movement, and rhythm. At his feet, Leconte de Lisle and Baudelaire made up two constellations of remarkable brilliance, and finding them together had been both a fascination and a love for us. Today's youth, positivist and narrow, practicing politics, studying market figures, and reading George Ohnet, would have trouble understanding the holy rapture with which we received our initiation into this new art, which in France at the beginning of the Second Empire had risen up out of the ruins of Romanticism like its final incarnation and was brought to us in poetry by the verses of Leconte de Lisle, Baudelaire, Coppée, Dierx, Mallarmé, and other lesser poets. And even less perhaps could understand such fervor those among the cultured youth who, already in their school years nourished on Spencer and Taine, anxiously and sharply seek to practice criticism, whereas we, more ingenuous and ardent, had given ourselves over to emotion. Even I find myself smiling today when I think of those nights in J. Teixeira de Azevedo's rooms, when I would fill two canons living next door with alarm and doubts by breaking the early morning hours with a declamation of Baudelaire's "Une Charogne," trembling and pale with passion:

Et pourtant vous serez semblable à cette ordure,
À cette horrible infection,
Étoile de mes yeux, soleil de ma nature,
Vous, mon ange et ma passion![2]

From the other side of the wall we could hear the creak of the ecclesiasts' beds, the terrified striking of matches. And I grew paler, with trembling ecstasy:

Alors, ô ma beauté, dites à la vermine
Qui vous mangera de baisers,
Que j'ai gardé la forme et l'essence divine,
De mes amours décomposés![3]

Baudelaire, of course, didn't deserve all that trembling and pallor. There is an essential beauty, however, in every sincere cult, regardless of the merits of the god for whom it flies up. Two hands clutched together in true faith are always touching, even when they are lifted up to a saint as vain and artificial as Saint Simeon Stylites. But our rapture was innocent and genuinely born of the fulfilled Ideal, comparable to the one in olden times that came over navigators from the Peninsula as they set foot on lands never before trod upon. Wondrous Eldorados, fertile with delights and treasures, where the pebbles on the beaches immediately looked to them like gleaming diamonds.

I read somewhere that Juan Ponce de León, bored with the dusty plains of

Old Castile and not finding any attraction either in the olive-green orchards of Andalusia, went to sea in search of other lands, wanting just to *mirar algo nuevo*.[4] For three years he plied uncertainly the melancholy Atlantic waters. He wandered for sad months lost in the mists of the Bermudas and all his hopes had sunk, so now he headed his battered prow toward where Spain had been left behind. But, behold! One fine sunny morning, on St. John's Day, before the ecstatic eyes of the fleet arose the splendors of Florida! "Gracias te sean dadas, mi San Juan bendito, que he mirado algo nuevo!"[5] The tears ran down his white beard and Juan Ponce de León died of emotion. We didn't die, but tears of the same type as those of the old sailor leaped from my eyes when for the first time I penetrated the somber glow and the bitter perfumes of *The Flowers of Evil*. That's how absurd we were in 1867!

In the end, just like Ponce de León I was simply searching in poetry and literature for *algo nuevo que mirar*. And for a twenty-year-old southern person, loving more than anything else color and sound in its full richness, what might that *algo nuevo* be if not the new splendor of these new forms? Form, the rare and unwritten beauty of Form, where in those times of delicate sensualism all my interest and all my care lay. Of course I worshipped the idea in its essence, but how much more the word that incarnated it! Baudelaire in "Une Charogne," showing his lover the rotting carcass of the dog, as he compared in both the miseries of the flesh, was a magnificent revelation and rapture for me. And before this taut and tormented subtilization of feeling, what was old and easy Lamartine worth with his "Lake," where he shows Elvira the weary moon and compares in both their pallor and their gentle grace? But if this harsh and funereal spirituality of Baudelaire had come to me in the soft, lax language of Casimir Delavigne, I wouldn't have paid any more attention to it than to the cheap verses in the *Almanaque de Lembranças*.

It was while I was sensually deep in such idolatry of form that I came upon those *Inscriptions* of Fradique Mendes where, joined together and melded, were the discordant qualities of majesty and nervous energy that constituted, or so it seemed to me, the grandeur of my two idols, the author of *The Flowers of Evil* and the author of the *Barbarous Poems*. Added to this and fascinating to me was the fact that this poet was Portuguese, carving out in that delightful way the language which until then had held as acclaimed jewels the "Betrothment of the Tomb" and the "Ave Caesar"![6] He lived in Lisbon, he was one of the "Novos," and he must have possessed in his soul, in his life perhaps, as much originality as in his poems. And that dog-eared copy of the *Revolução de Setembro* thus took on the importance of a revelation in art, a dawn of poetry coming into birth to bathe young souls in the light and special warmth to which they aspired, half-asleep and almost frozen under the chilling moonlight of Romanticism. Thanks be to you, my blessed Fradique, in my ancient tongue *he mirado algo nuevo*! I think I whispered that, bathed in gratitude. And, carrying the copy of the *Revolução de Setembro*, I ran to J. Teixeira de Azevedo's on the Travessa do Guarda-Mor to announce that splendid advent.

I found him as usual, lost in his silent summer afternoon musings, in shirt-sleeves, over a bowl overflowing with strawberries and Torres wine. Shouting and waving my arms toward the ceiling, I declaimed "The Death of the Saint" to him. If memory serves, that ascetic, coming to his end in the snows of Silesia, had been miserably betrayed by a disloyal Nature. All the appetites of passion and the body, so laboriously held in check over his half a century as a hermit, were suddenly bursting forth on the edge of eternity in a bestial tumult, refusing to end forever with the flesh that was coming to its end without being satisfied once and for all. And the angels coming to receive him, with palm fronds under their arms and singing the Epithalamia, found instead of a saint a satyr, senile and grotesque, who was crawling, growling, and biting the snow with voracious kisses, the smooth whiteness of the snow where his delirium was furiously imagining the nakedness of courtesans . . . All this was treated with a primitive and sober grandeur that seemed sublime to me. J. Texeira de Azevedo also found it sublime if a bit trashy. But he agreed that it would be proper to remove Fradique Mendes from the waste bin of obscurity and raise him up on the shield as the radiant master of the New.

I went that very night to the *Revolução de Setembro*, to look up a schoolmate of mine from Coimbra, Marcos Vidigal, who in our happy days of reading Roman and Canon Law had amassed, from playing the accordion, reading the *History of Music* by Scudo, and dropping all over the Academy the names of Mozart and Beethoven, a reputation as a superb authority on classical music. Now, loafing about in Lisbon, on Sundays he was writing a "Lyrical Chronicle" in the *Revolução* in order to get a free pass to the São Carlos.

He was a young man with thinning hair the color of butter and freckled skin, dull when it came to ideas and style, but who came awake and lighted up at every "chance"—as he put it—"of rubbing against a famous person or of getting involved in something original." And that had slowly turned him, bit by bit, into someone almost original and almost famous. On that night of a hot oppressive Saturday, there he was on his bench, wearing an alpaca jacket, sweating, snorting, and squeezing out of his poor cranium, the way you would juice from a half-squeezed lemon, the drops of a chronicle on La Volpini. No sooner did I mention Fradique Mendes and the poetry that had captivated me so than Vidigal threw down his pen, smiling now with a glow dawning across his pudgy face.

"Fradique? Do you know the great Fradique? He's my kinsman, my countryman, my partner!"

"That's wonderful, Vidigal, that's wonderful!"

We went to the Passeio Público (where Marcos was to meet a loan shark). We had some sherbet under the acacias and it was from the columnist for the *Revolução* that I got to know about the origins, youth, and accomplishments of the poet of the *Inscriptions*.

Carlos Fradique Mendes belonged to an old and wealthy family from the Azores. On his father's side, he was descended from the navigator Dom Lopo Mendes, the second son of the House of Troba and the recipient of one of the first captaincies created on the islands in the sixteenth century. His father, a magnificently handsome man but with coarse tastes, had died in a hunting accident when Carlos was still crawling on his hands and knees. Six years later, his mother, a lady so haughty, pensive, and blonde that a poet from the island of Terceira nicknamed her a "Virgin out of Ossian," also died, from a fever contracted in the fields where she strolled bucolically, singing and cutting hay, on a day when there was strong sun. Carlos was left in the care of his maternal grandmother, Dona Angelina Fradique, a reckless, erudite, and exotic old lady who collected stuffed birds, translated Klopstock, and suffered perpetually from the "arrows of love." His early education was singularly tangled. Dona Angelina's chaplain, a former Benedictine monk, taught him Latin, doctrine, a horror of Freemasonry, and other sound principles. Then a French colonel, a strict Jacobin who had fought on the barricades of Saint-Merri in 1830, arrived to knock down those spiritual foundations, making the boy translate Voltaire's *Pucelle* as well as the *Declaration of the Rights of Man*. And, lastly, it was a German who was helping Dona Angelina dress Klopstock up in the vernacular of Filinto Elísio and claimed to be a relative of Immanuel Kant who completed the confusion by initiating Carlos, before his first growth of beard, in the *Critique of Pure Reason* and the metaphysical heterodoxies of the professors at Tübingen. Fortunately, by then Carlos had taken a liking to spending long days in the countryside on horseback, along with his small pack of greyhounds, and he was saved from the anemia that the abstractions of reason might have brought on by the cool breath of the oak groves and the pure nature of the brooklets from which he drank.

His grandmother, having impartially approved of these entangled lines of his education, suddenly decided, when Carlos had turned sixteen, to send him to

Coimbra, which she considered a noble center of classical studies and the last refuge of the Humanities. Talk on the island, however, had it that the translator of Klopstock, in spite of the sixty years that covered her face with hair thicker than the ivy of ruins, had decided to send her grandson away in order to marry the coachman.

For three years, Carlos played the guitar in the Penedo da Saudade, drowned in the rotgut wine served by the Camelas sisters in their tavern, published ascetic sonnets in *A Ideia*, and fell desperately in love with the daughter of a blacksmith in Lorvão. He had just failed Geometry when his grandmother suddenly died on her estate, As Tornas, in a rose bower where she had dozed off for a siesta in June, while sipping coffee and listening to the guitar the coachman was plucking with fingers that were loaded down with rings.

Carlos was left with an uncle, Tadeu Mendes, a man of luxury and a good table who lived in Paris, preparing the salvation of society with Persigny, Morny, and Prince Louis Napoleon, of whom he was a devoted follower and a creditor. So Carlos went to Paris to study Law in the beer halls surrounding the Sorbonne as he waited for his majority, which was to bring him the accumulated inheritances from his father and his grandmother, calculated by Vidigal to be a fat million cruzados. Vidigal was the son of a niece of Dona Angelina's. He had been born on the island of Terceira and as a legacy owned, together with Carlos, an estate called Corcovelo. Out of that he came to be the "kinsman, countryman, and partner" of the man of the *Inscriptions*.

All that Vidigal knew after this was that Fradique was free and rich and that he had left the Latin Quarter to begin a superb and wild existence. With the impetus of a freed bird, he traveled all over the world at full sail, from Chicago to Jerusalem, from Iceland to the Sahara. On these journeys, always undertaken because of an intellectual drive or from an emotional yearning, he found himself in the midst of historic deeds and dealing with outstanding people of the century. Wearing a red shirt, he had accompanied Garibaldi in his conquest of the Two Sicilies. Serving on the general staff of old Napier, who called him the "Portuguese Lion," he had taken part in the Abyssinian campaign. He got letters from Mazzini. Just months ago he had visited Hugo on his crags in Guernsey . . .

Here I fell back, wide-eyed. Victor Hugo (everyone still remembers), exiled at the time on Guernsey, held for us idealists and democrats of 1867 the sublime and legendary proportions of a Saint John on Patmos. And I drew back in protest, eyes inflamed, so much it seemed to me beyond the realm of possibilities that a Portuguese, a Mendes, could have held in his the august hand that had written *The Legend of the Centuries*! Corresponding with Mazzini, camaraderie with Garibaldi, that was all very well! But a sojourn on that sacred isle, to the sound of the waves from the Channel, strolling, chatting, pondering with the sage of *Les Misérables*, looked to me like the impudent exaggerations of an Azorean islander who was trying to put one over on me . . .

"I swear it!" Vidigal shouted, raising his hand up to the acacias above us, as if in an oath.

And immediately, in order to demonstrate the singularity of that glory, already at its peak for Fradique, he told me about another quite superior one, which encircled that unusual man with a gleaming halo. Now it wasn't a matter of his being esteemed by an outstanding man, but rather, something delightful among so many other things, that fact that he had been loved by an outstanding woman. Yes indeed! For two years in Paris Fradique had been the chosen one of Ana de Léon, the glorious Ana de Léon, the most cultured and beautiful courtesan (Vidigal said "the most delicious mouthful") of the Second Empire, of which she, through the unique grace of her intelligent voluptuosity, like Aspasia in the age of Pericles, had been the muse and flower.

Many times had I read in *Le Figaro* the praises of Ana de Léon and I knew that poets had celebrated her under the name of the "Conquering Venus." Fradique's love affair with the courtesan had not impressed me as much, of course, as his intimacy with the man of the *Contemplations*. But my disbelief ended and Fradique took on for me the stature of one of those people who through seduction or genius, like Alcibiades or Goethe, dominate a civilization and from it delightfully pluck everything it has to give in the way of pleasures and triumphs.

It was for that reason perhaps that I blushed when Vidigal, ordering another milk sherbet, offered to take me to meet the remarkable Fradique. Indecisive, thinking of Novalis who also hesitated like that, perplexed one morning in Berlin, as he mounted the steps to Hegel's home, I asked Vidigal if the poet of the *Inscriptions* lived in Lisbon. No indeed! Fradique had only just arrived from England to visit Sintra, which he loved and where on the road to Capuchos he had bought an estate called Saragoça in order to have a summer place in Portugal worthy of the leisure of a nobleman. He had been there since Saint Anthony's Day and was stopping in Lisbon now at the Hotel Central before returning to Paris, his center of activity where he had his home. Also, Marcos went on, there was no one as down-to-earth, jolly, or as easygoing as Fradique. And if I wanted to meet a man of genius I should wait the following day, Sunday, by the door of the Casa Havanesa after the two o'clock mass at the Loreto church.

"All set? Two o'clock sharp, after the mass."

My heart was pounding. Finally, making an effort, like Novalis at Hegel's doorstep, I gave my word, paying for the sherbet. The next day at two o'clock sharp, religiously but without attending mass, I would be at the door of the Havanesa.

II

I spent the night putting together phrases filled with depth and beauty to lay before Fradique Mendes, all of them tending toward a glorification of the *Inscriptions*. I remember having chiseled out and polished this one with loving care: "Your form, sir, is a piece of divine marble that has a human tremor."

That morning I took great care with my appearance, as though instead of Fradique I would be meeting Ana de Léon—with whom, in an early-morning dream full of erudition and sensibility, I had been strolling along the sacred road from Athens to Eleusis, conversing among the lilies we were plucking about Plato's teachings and the versification of the *Inscriptions*. And at two o'clock, in a cab, so that the wet pavement wouldn't dull my polished shoes, I stopped at the Havanesa, pale, perfumed, and excited, with a huge tea rose in my lapel. That was the way we were in 1867!

Marcos Vidigal was already there waiting for me, impatient and chewing on his cigar. He jumped into the cab and we went off through Loreto, under the scorching August sun.

On the Rua do Alecrim (in order to get rid of the puerile emotion that was making me all confused), I asked my companion when Fradique was going to publish the *Inscriptions*. Over the clatter of the wheels Vidigal shouted:

"Never!"

And he told me how the publication of those excerpts in the *Revolução de Setembro* had almost brought on "an intellectual dogfight" between him and Fradique. One day after lunch in Sintra, while Fradique was smoking his Persian chibouk, Vidigal, in his capacity of fellow countryman and relative, had opened up a black velvet portfolio on the table. With surprise, he came upon a sheaf of some pages with poetry, written in now faded ink on yellowing paper. It was the *Inscriptions*. He read the first one, "Satan's Serenade to the Stars," and, entranced by it, he asked Fradique to let them publish some of those divine stanzas in the *Revolução*. His cousin smiled and agreed, but under the firm condition that they be signed with a pseudonym. What one? . . . Fradique left that up to

Vidigal's fantasy. At the paper, however, as he checked the proofs, the only pseudonyms that came to mind were lame and silly: the Independent, the Friend of Truth, the Observer, none of them new enough to be worthy of being signed under such new poetry. He said to himself, "Enough! Sublimity is nothing to be ashamed of. I'm going to use his name." But when Fradique saw the *Revolução de Setembro* he was livid and he icily called Vidigal "indiscreet, bourgeois, philistine"—and here Vidigal stopped to ask me the meaning of "philistine." I didn't know, but I greedily filed the term away as something bitter. I even remember that already the same afternoon, at Martinho, I called the eminent author of "Ave Caesar" a philistine.

"So," Vidigal concluded, "it would be best if you didn't bring up the *Inscriptions* with him."

Yes, I thought, maybe Fradique, like Chancellor Bacon and other great men of action, wishes to hide his delicate poetic genius from this world of materialism and force. Or perhaps his anger at seeing his name in print under verses of which Leconte de Lisle would have been proud may be that of a noble and perpetually dissatisfied artist who cannot accept laying before people as his a piece of work where he senses imperfections. This manner of being, so superior and so new, fell onto my admiration like oil onto a fire. As we stopped at the Central I was trembling with timidity.

I felt relief when the doorman announced that early that morning Mr. Fradique Mendes had taken a *calèche* to Belém. Vidigal was pale with despair.

"A *calèche* to Belém! Is there anything in Belém?"

I mumbled something about art, that the Jerónimos Monastery was there. At that moment a worn-out carriage came down the street; the nags pulling it were steaming with sweat. A man got out, briskly and athletically. It was Fradique Mendes.

Vidigal, all excited, introduced me as "a poet friend of his." Fradique put out his hand, smiling. It was a delicate white hand where a ruby gleamed its red. Then, patting his cousin Marcos on the shoulder, he opened a letter that the doorman handed him.

Then I was able to take my time in contemplating the sculptor of the *Inscriptions*, the close friend of Mazzini, the conqueror of the Two Sicilies, the lover of Ana de Léon. What immediately attracted me was his splendid, solid shape, the healthy, manly size of his limbs, his calm look of powerful stability that he seemed to be giving to life so freely and so firmly as over the brick pavement his long, polished shoes gleamed under his linen spats. His face had the aquiline and graceful lines that are called Caesarian, but without the plaster look and flaccid thickness which traditional schools invariably attribute to the Caesars on the canvas or in plaster, so as to endow them with a majestic aspect. Instead, his face was pure and delicately drawn, like that of a young Lucretius in full glory, all involved in dreams of virtue and art. On the fresh, milk-white skin of his chin, a close shave had not left even a trace of any roughness or shadow. On the fringe of his lips, whose moist red tint and subtle twist seemed to have been masterfully carved to accommodate equally well both irony and love, there was a thin, curly fuzz. And all his refinement, mingled with energy, was in his eyes: small and dark, gleaming like onyx beads, with a sharp and perhaps too insistent penetration that could pierce and bury itself effortlessly, like a steel drill penetrating soft wood.

He was wearing a light double-breasted jacket of a soft black fabric, the same as that of his trousers, which fell without a wrinkle. His white linen waistcoat was closed with some light coral buttons, and the knot in his black satin cravat gave relief to the shiny lift of the wings of his collar. All of this presented me with the same gift of concise perfection that had already enchanted me in his poetry.

I don't know whether or not women considered him *handsome*. I found him to cut a magnificent male figure—dominating, especially, with the clear grace that came out of all his masculine strength. It was his vigor that was dazzling. A life of such varied and arduous activities had not carved out any wrinkles of fatigue. He seemed to have emerged, just moments before, in his black jacket and clean-shaven, from the living depths of nature. And in spite of Vidigal's having told me that Fradique had celebrated his "thirty-third" in Sintra on Saint Peter's Day, I sensed in that body the tender and agile robustness of an ephebe in the infancy of the Greek world. Only when he smiled or looked at something would one immediately catch in him twenty centuries of literature.

After reading the letter, Fradique threw up his arms in a smiling gesture of desolation, asking for Vidigal's pity. It was a matter, as always, of Customs, the perennial source of his bitter moments. Stranded there now was a crate containing an Egyptian mummy . . .

"A mummy?"

Yes, and, precisely, a historic mummy, the genuine and venerable body of Pentaur, a priestly scribe of the temple of Amon in Thebes, Ramses II's chronicler. He had ordered it from Paris, in order to give it to a woman at the British legation, Lady Mary Ross, a friend of his from Athens, who with thoroughgoing impudence and good luck collected funerary antiquities from Egypt and Assyria . . . But in spite of astute efforts, he had been unable to extract the defunct man of letters from the Customs warehouse, which he had filled with confusion and horror. On the very first afternoon, when Pentaur had disembarked all wrapped up and in his casket, Customs, terrified, had called in the police. Later on, when suspicions of a crime had been satisfied, an insurmountable difficulty had arisen: what tariff covered the corpse of a hierographer from the time of Ramses? He, Fradique, had suggested the article that taxed smoked herring. Really, when you come down to it, what is a smoked herring but the mummy, without wrappings or inscriptions, of a fish that had once been alive? Whether a fish or a scribe was of no concern from a fiscal point of view. What Customs had before it was the body of a creature that once had had a beating heart and today was dried out as in a smokehouse. Whether in life it used to swim in a school under the waves of the North Sea or sat by the banks of the Nile four thousand years ago, listing Amon's cattle and commenting on the day's events, it was certainly not the business of the authorities. This seemed quite logical to him. And yet the Customs people continued hesitant, scratching their chins alongside the vari-colored casket that encased so much knowledge and so much piety. Now, in that letter, his friends the Pintos Bastos were advising him that the quickest and most patriotic way was to obtain a pledge drawn up by the Minister of the Treas-ury allowing the release without duty of the august body of Ramses's scribe. Who was better suited to get this pledge than Marcos, the mainstay of *Revolução* and its musical chronicler?

Vidigal rubbed his hands, illuminated. It was something quite worthy for him, the rescue of the mummy of a "great Pharaonic figure" from the tax col-lector, something "quite elegant." And he snatched the letter from the Pintos Bastos, jumped into the carriage, shouted to the coachman the address of the Minister, his colleague on the *Revolução de Setembro*, and I was left behind alone with Fradique, who invited me up to his rooms to wait for Vidigal and have some soda with lemon.

On the stairs, the poet of the *Inscriptions* mentioned the torrid August heat. And I, who at that moment was facing the mirror on the landing and furtively checking the cut of my frock coat and the freshness of my rose, came out with this rattle-brained bit of downright foolishness:

"Yes, it's enough to split a person in two."

And before the silly sound of it had died out, I was being lashed by affliction over that clumsy comment, worthy of a corner tobacconist, so carelessly thrown out like a wad of grease at the supreme artist of the *Inscriptions*, the man who had chatted by the sea with Hugo! . . . I entered the room giddy and with drops of sweat on my forehead, uselessly seeking out some kind of phrase about the heat that would be elaborate, something all sparkling and new. Nothing! Everything that came to me was equally clumsy, insistent slang. "It's abusive!" "You feel like a crushed pineapple!" "It melts all your juices!" . . . I went through one of those bits of atrocious and grotesque anxiety, which at the age of twenty, when life and literature begin, furrow the soul and are never forgotten.

Fradique had fortunately disappeared behind the drapes of an alcove. Left alone, wiping my brow, feeling that great thinkers express themselves like that, with crude simplicity, I calmed down. And I followed my distress with curiosity as I searched everywhere, through the apartment, to find around me some vestige of the intense originality of the man who lived there. But all I saw were some tired blue repp chairs, a chandelier wrapped in tulle, and a console table with long gilded legs that stood between two windows facing the river. Except that on the marble top on the console and in the midst of books piled up on an old blackwood table, some superb bouquets of flowers were perched. And in a corner, there was a wide divan that stood out, arranged by Fradique, of course, overstuffed and draped with two oriental blankets in strident colors. Along with this, there was a wafting about all through the room, an unknown odor that also seemed oriental to me, like that of roses from Smyrna mingled with a touch of cinnamon and marjoram.

Fradique Mendes came out wearing a Chinese tunic, a mandarin's tunic of green silk embroidered with almond blossoms, which startled and intimidated me. I saw then that he had dark, brown hair, wispy and slightly curled over his forehead, which was smoother and whiter than ivory work from Normandy. And his eyes, bathed now in a bright light, didn't show that deep darkness which I had compared to onyx, but were the warm color of dark Havana tobacco. He lighted a cigarette and ordered some "lemon and soda" from a rather strange-looking servant, quite blond and quite solemn, with a pearl stickpin in his necktie, who wore ample trousers with a black and green checkered pattern and on whose chest three yellow carnations bloomed! (I discovered later that his name was Smith.) My confusion kept growing, and, finally, Fradique said softly, smiling and with sincere affection:

"That Marcos is a delightful fellow!"

I agreed and I told him of my great esteem for Vidigal ever since our first year at Coimbra, of our wild days with a concertina and lecture notes. Then, happily recalling Coimbra, Fradique asked me about Pedro Penedo, Pais, and other professors of that old monkish and coarse kind, and then about the Camelas, those enchanting old ladies who, generation after generation of lascivious students, had scrupulously remained virgins in order to be able to sit beside Saint

Cecilia in Heaven and spend an eternity plucking the harp . . . One of his best memories of Coimbra was that of the Camelas tavern and the huge dinners that cost seventy réis, eaten noisily in the smoky half-light with a plate of sardines on your knees, in the midst of fierce battles over metaphysics and art. And what sardines! Such a divine art in the frying of fish! Many times in Paris he would remember the laughter, the illusions, and the tidbits of those days . . .

All of this was coming out in a quite youthful, sincere, and simple tone, which I mentally classified as *crystalline*. He had stretched out on the divan and I remained by the table where, because of the heat, a bouquet of roses was shedding its petals over volumes by Darwin and Father Manuel Bernardes. And then, having lost my shyness, filled with an appetite for the discussion of some literary ideas with that man of genius, and forgetting that, like Bacon, he might wish to hide his poetic genius, or that an unsatisfied artist would never recognize an imperfect piece of work, I mentioned the *Inscriptions*.

Fradique Mendes took the cigarette out of his mouth and laughed laughter that would have seemed genuinely jolly if he hadn't betrayed a touch of blush rising up across his milky white face. Then he declared that the publication of those verses over his signature had been a bit of treachery by the frivolous Marcos. He didn't consider as "autographable" those pieces of rhymed prose in which fifteen years ago, at the age when one imitates, he had copied some poetry of Leconte de Lisle. It had been during a summer of work and faith in a garret overlooking the Luxembourg, as he thought that with every rhyme he was an innovator of genius.

I hastened to their defense, all worked up and stating that after Baudelaire nothing in art had impressed me as much as the *Inscriptions*. And I was about to come out with my splendid phrase chiseled out with patient care the night before: "Your form is a divine piece of marble . . ." But Fradique had risen from the divan and was resting his delicate onyx eyes on me with a curiosity that bored right through me.

"So I see," he said, "that you're a devotee of that scoundrel of *The Flowers of Evil*."

I blushed at that horrible term of *scoundrel*. And I confessed very solemnly that Baudelaire for me dominated modern poetry like a great star, right under Hugo. Then Fradique, smiling paternally, wagered that I would lose that illusion rather soon. Baudelaire (whom he had met) was not really a poet. Poetry presumed emotion and Baudelaire, all intellect, didn't go beyond being a psychologist, an analyst, a subtle dissector of morbid states. *The Flowers of Evil* contained nothing but critical summaries of moral tortures that Baudelaire had very keenly understood but had never personally *felt*. His work was like that of a pathologist whose heart beats normally and calmly as he describes at his desk, on a sheet of paper and after an accumulation of erudition and observation, the fearful disturbances of a cardiac lesion. So much so that Baudelaire had first composed *The Flowers of Evil* in prose, and only later, after rectifying the accuracy of his analyses, did he turn them into verse, laboriously and with the help of a rhyming dictionary! Furthermore, this unique man added, there were no poets in France. The true expression for clear French intelligence was prose. The country's most refined connoisseurs always preferred poets whose poetry was characterized by precision, lucidity, and sobriety, which are qualities of prose, and a poet became the more popular the more visibly he possessed the qualities of a prose writer. Boileau will still be a classic and an immortal when no one in France remembers the tumultuous lyricism of Hugo anymore . . .

He was stating those tremendous things in a slow, penetrating voice, one that carved out the terms with certainty and with the perfection of a chisel. And I was listening, thunderstruck! That a Boileau, a pedagogue, a court jester, would remain at the summit of French poetry with his "Ode to the Conquest of Namur," his wig, and his stick, while the name of the poet of *The Legend of the Centuries* would evaporate like the breath of a passing breeze, seemed to me one of those statements of extravagant originality with which one tries to astonish simpletons and which I mentally classified as insolent. I had a thousand abundant and crushing things with which to respond, but I didn't dare, unable to present them in that translucid and geometric form of the poet of the *Inscriptions*. That cowardice of mine, however, and the effort to restrain the protests of my enthusiasm for the masters of my youth muffled me, made me uneasy, and I was only anxious to flee that room where with such moldy classical opinions, along with all the roses in vases and the soft scents of cinnamon and marjoram that I was breathing in, there was also the stifling air of the seraglio and the academy.

At the same time, I considered it humiliating that in conversation with the close friend of Mazzini and Hugo I had come out only with some brief comments on Pedro Penedo and the strong wine of the Camelas. And with a proper wish to dazzle Fradique with some critical comment that proved my refined culture, I resorted to the phrase, the chiseled phrase, about the form of his poetry. Smiling and twisting my mustache, I said softly, "In any case, your form is like a work in marble . . ." Suddenly the door opened and Vidigal burst in shouting:

"Everything's all set. I took care of the deceased!"

The minister, a man of poetry and eloquence, had taken a generous interest in that mummy of a "colleague" and had sworn immediately that he would be spared the ignominy of being taxed as a salted fish. His Excellency had even added, "No, sir! No sir! He is to enter freely, with all the honors due a classic!" And the first thing next morning Pentaur would leave Customs in a carriage.

Fradique laughed at that designation of a *classic* given to a scribe from the time of Ramses. And Vidigal triumphantly sat down at the piano and began playing the "Grand Duchess." Then, strangely overcome by an inexplicable feeling of inferiority and melancholy, I picked up my hat. Fradique didn't hold me back but accompanied me for the few steps to the hallway. His smile and his handshake were perfect. Only out on the street did I give vent to, "What a pedant!"

Yes, but someone completely *new*, so unlike all the men I'd met up till then. And that night, on the Travessa do Guarda-Mor (not mentioning his scandalous defense of Boileau so as not to reveal any imperfection in him), I startled J. Teixeira de Azevedo with an idealized Fradique in whom everything was irresistible: ideas, talk, silk tunic, the marble face of a young Lucretius, the perfume he'd spread about, the erudition, the charm, and the good taste!

Any enthusiasm on J. Teixeira's part was difficult and slow to light up. The man only gave him the impression of someone artificial and theatrical. He did agree, however, that it would be fitting to study "the mechanism of a pose that had been put together with so much luxury."

Later on, we both took a cab to the Central. I was wearing a satin tie and I had a gardenia on my lapel. J. Teixeira de Azevedo, in character as a "nineteenth-century Diogenes," carried a fearsome iron-tipped cudgel and wore a Braga cap fringed with sweat marks, a grimy, mended double-breasted coat that a servant had loaned him, and a pair of thick rustic shoes. All that had been put together with great care, effort, and with intense annoyance simply in order to horrify Fradique and to present, haughtily, before that man of skepticism and luxury, as a democrat and an idealist, the moral grandeur of the patches and the philosophical austerity of the stains. That's what we were like in 1867!

It was all in vain. My gardenia was in vain, my comrade's stoic filth was in vain. Mr. Fradique Mendes, the doorman said, had sailed that evening on a ship that was going to Morocco to pick up cattle.

III

A few years went by. I worked. I traveled. I was gaining a better knowledge of people and what things were really like. I'd lost my worship of form and hadn't gone back to reading Baudelaire. Marcos Vidigal, who by way of the *Revolução de Setembro* had risen from his music reporting to Civil Administration, was now governing India, as a Secretary General. In the idle moments that the State offered him in Asia, he'd gone back to his *History of Music* and his concertina. So with that pleasant friend borne off from the Tagus to the Mandovi I heard nothing more about the poet of the *Inscriptions*. But the memory of that singular man had never been erased from my mind. Rather, it would sometimes suddenly happen that I would see, see quite clearly, standing out and almost tangible, that cool, ivory face of his, those piercing tobacco-brown eyes, and his sinuous, skeptical smile where twenty centuries of literature were alive.

In 1871 I was traveling about Egypt. On one occasion in Memphis (or at the spot where Memphis used to be), I was sailing along the flooded banks of the Nile, by palm trees that emerged from the waters and reproduced under a radiant oriental moon the sad and contemplative solemnity of the long archways of a monastery. It was the solitude of a vast silence of dead earth, softly broken only by the cadence of the oars and the helmsman's mournful chant . . . And, behold, all of a sudden and with no memory of anything before that might have evoked that image, there I *see*, clearly *see*, sailing along with the boat and cutting through the bands of light and shadow, the room in the Hotel Central, the large divan with its gaudy colors, and Fradique in his silk tunic celebrating the immortality of Boileau in the midst of cigarette smoke! And I myself was no longer in the East or in Memphis, on the unmoving waters of the Nile, but there, among the blue repp chairs, under the tulle-wrapped chandelier, facing the two windows that opened onto the Tagus and hearing from below the wagons with iron goods rolling toward the Arsenal. I had lost the shyness that had held me back that time, however, and while we were rowing along through the Pharaonic scenery to the home of Sheikh Abu-Kair, I was arguing with the poet of the *Inscriptions* and finally speaking out in defense of Hugo and Baudelaire, with all the subtle and momentous things I had to be mute about on that August afternoon. The helmsman was singing about the groves of Damascus and I was mentally shouting, "But sir, look at the high moral lesson in *Les Misérables* . . . !"

The next day, which was the feast of Beiram, I returned to Cairo during the hottest time, when the muezzins chant the third prayer. And as I was dismounting from my donkey in front of Shepheard's Hotel, in the Ezbekieh gardens, whom did I catch sight of? What man among all men did I spot there on the terrace, stretched out on a wicker chaise-longue with his hands crossed behind his neck and the *Times* lying forgotten on his knees, as he soaked up all the heat and light, but Fradique Mendes!

I bounded up the terrace steps calling out Fradique's name with a laugh that overflowed with pleasure. Without ruffling his beatific pose, he simply unfolded one arm and slowly held it out to me. The charm of his reception lay in the ease with which he recognized me through my dark glasses and my wide-brimmed Panama hat.

"So, how have you been since the Hotel Central? . . . How long are you in Cairo?"

He spoke a few more indolent and affable words. As I sat down on a bench close by, I was all smiles and I was brushing off the dust that had covered my face with the thickness of a mask. During the short and sweet moment that we chatted, I learned that Fradique had arrived from Suez the week before, coming from the banks of the Euphrates and from Persia, where he had roamed as in a fairy tale for a whole year and a day. He said he had a *debarieh* with the beautiful name of *Rose of the Waters* and a crew, all prepared to sail, tied up at the Bulak docks. He was taking it up the Nile, all the way to Nubia, even beyond Ibsambul . . .

All that sun above the Red Sea and the plains of the Euphrates had not tanned his milk-white skin. Exactly the same as at the Hotel Central, he was wearing a wide black jacket and a white vest with coral buttons. And the knot in his black satin tie was a very good representative of the formal precision of Western ideas in that land of loose, bright-colored garments.

He asked me about easy-going Lisbon and about Vidigal, who was attending to his bureaucratic duties among Brahmanic palm trees . . . Then, as I kept wiping off the sweat and the dust, he advised me to purify myself in a Turkish bath, in a pool that was near the El Moayed mosque, and to rest all afternoon so that at night we could take in the lights of Beiram.

But instead of resting after the purifying bath I still set out to the soft trot of a donkey through the hot dust of the Libyan Desert to visit the tombs of the Caliphs outside Cairo. That night, as I was sitting down in the dining room of the Shepheard's over some ox-tail soup, fatigue began to take away the desire to be amazed at any other Muslim wonders. What was attracting me was the cool bed in my matting-covered room, where the fountains in the garden could be heard singing so romantically among the rosebushes.

Fradique Mendes was already dining at a table where the branch of a huge cactus stood out against the lights. Seated beside him on a Moorish bench was a lady dressed in white, of whom I could only catch the splendid mass of her blonde hair and her perfect, graceful back, like that of a statue by Praxiteles which happened to wear a halter by Madame Marcel. Across from her, spread out in an armchair, was a flabby, fat man whose broad face with its curly beard was filled with the tranquil strength of the face of a Jupiter I must have come across somewhere, either alive or in marble. And I immediately fell to wondering. On what street, in what museum had I admired that Olympian face, where only the fatigue of looking out from under the heavy eyelids betrayed mortal clay?

I ended up asking the black waiter from Seneh, who was serving the macaroni. The savage opened up a wide and sparkling white laugh across the ebony of his round face and grunted respectfully from across the table, "*Cé-le-dieu . . .*" Good Lord! *Le Dieu*! Was the black man telling me that that man with the curly beard *was a god*? The very special and well-known god who was living at the Shepheard's! Had it been on an altar, then, on some devotional painting, that I had seen that face, majestically enhanced by the perpetual absorption of incense and prayer? I questioned the Nubian again when he returned bearing a steaming platter in his stretched-out hands. Once more the Nubian threw out to me in clear and resonant words, removing any doubt or uncertainty, "*C'est le Dieu!*"

He was a god! I smiled at that idea out of literature: a god in a dinner jacket dining at a table at Shepheard's. And little by little, there came floating out of my weary imagination a kind of dream, sparse and thin, like the smoke rising from a half-extinguished brazier. It was about Olympus, the old gods, and that friend of Fradique's that looked like Jupiter. Maybe the gods, I mused (picking up forkfuls of tomato salad), hadn't died but ever since the arrival of Saint Paul in Greece had been living as refugees in a valley in Laconia, given over once more, with the leisure that the new God had imposed on them, to their primordial occupations of farmers and shepherds. Except that, either from the habit the gods had never lost of imitating men or in order to escape the outrages of a shameful Christianity, the Olympians were muffling under skirts and greatcoats the splendor of the nudity that Antiquity had worshipped. And since they were taking on other human customs, either out of necessity (every day it becomes more and more difficult to be a god) or out of curiosity (every day it becomes more and more fun to be a man), the gods were slowly becoming accustomed to their humanization. From time to time now, they would leave the sweetness of their bucolic valley and with trunks and carpet bags would travel for business or for pleasure, thumbing through Baedeker guidebooks. Some went to study, in cities, the civilized wonders of press, parliamentarianism, and gas; others, counseled by the erudite Hermes, would cut short the monotony of the long summers of Attica by drinking the waters of Vichy or Carlsbad; others still, with the everlasting nostalgia of past omnipotence would make pilgrimages to the ruins of temples where in days gone by they had been offered honey and the blood of livestock. Therefore, it was quite likely that the man there whose face full of majesty and serene force was reproducing the features with which Jupiter had revealed himself to the School of Athens really was Jupiter, the Thunderer, the Fecund, the inexhaustible Father of the Gods, the creator of Law and Order. But what reason could have brought him there, dressed in blue flannel, to Cairo, to Shepheard's, eating a dish of macaroni that was profanely clinging to the beard over which ambrosia had once flowed? It surely must have been the sweet reasons that throughout Antiquity, in Heaven and on Earth, had always inspired the actions of Jupiter, Jupiter the lecherous, Jupiter the dissolute. What else could have dragged him to Cairo if not some *skirt*, with that splendidly insatiable desire for goddesses and for women, which in other times had made the maidens of Hellenia pensive as they memorized from their pagan primers the dates on which he had flapped his swan's wings between Leda's knees, shaken his bull's horns between Europa's arms, dripped golden droplets onto the breasts of Danae, pushed his tongues of flame between the lips of Aegina, and even one day, irking Minerva and the proper ladies of Olympus, crossed all of Macedonia with a ladder on his shoulder to clamber up to dark Semele's high balcony? Now he was evidently spending a few sentimental vacation days, far away from the sluggish and conjugal Juno, with that exuberant woman whose irresistible bust had its origins in the joint artistic skills of Praxiteles and Madame Marcel. But she, who could she be? The color of her tresses, the soft flowing lines of her shoulders, everything clearly indicated one of those delightful nymphs from the isles of Ionia whom Christian deacons in times gone by had expelled from their cool brooklets, in order to baptize there cachectic centurions eaten away by debt or old maidens with hairs on their chins who were hobbling from their incessant pilgrimages to the altars of Aphrodite. Neither he nor she, however, could hide their divine origins. The nymph's body glowed through her muslin dress and if one paid careful attention one could see Jupiter's marble brow throbbing rhythmically in his calm work of perpetually conceiving Law and Order.

But what about Fradique? How did Fradique come to be there in the intimacy of the Immortals, drinking Clicquot champagne with them and listening from close by to the ineffable harmony of Jove's words? Fradique was one of the last believers in Olympus, devoutly prostrate before Form and overflowing with pagan joy. He had visited Laconia. He spoke the language of the gods. He received his inspiration from them. It was quite natural that he should find Jupiter in Cairo and immediately attach himself to his service as his guide in the barbarian lands of Allah. And it was surely with him and with the nymph from Ionia that Fradique would be going up the Nile on the *Rose of the Waters*, to the tumble-down temples where Jupiter would probably whisper, thoughtful, and pointing out the ruined altars with the tip of his umbrella, "I used to be offered a lot of incense here."

So it was that through my tomato salad I went on developing and coordinating those bits of imagination and decided to convert them into a story to publish in Lisbon in the *Gazeta de Portugal.* I would call it "Jupiter's Last Campaign," and in it I would lay down a base of erudition and fantasy on which I could inlay all my notes on customs and countryside garnered on my trip to Egypt. Except that, in order to give the story a touch of modernism and spicy realism, I would have the water nymph on that journey up the Nile fall in love with Fradique and betray Jupiter! And there she would be, taking advantage of every corner of the palm grove and every shadow cast by the ancient columns of Osiris to hang her arms around the neck of the poet of the *Inscriptions*, whispering things in Greek that were sweeter than the verses of Hesiod, leaving her scent of ambrosia on his flannel suit, and acting, all along the valley of the Nile, immensely *cochonne*, while the father of the gods, stroking his curly beard, would go along imperturbably creating Order, supreme, august, perfect, ancestral, and cuckolded!

All enthused, I was already putting together the first line of the story: "It was in Cairo, in the gardens of Chubra, after the Ramadan fast . . . ,"—when I saw Fradique coming over to me, his coffee cup in his hand. Jupiter had also gotten up, wearily. To me he looked like a heavy, sluggish god, with the beginnings of obesity and dragging his clumsy leg, quite in line with the outrage I was preparing for him in the *Gazeta de Portugal.* She, however, had the harmony, the aroma, the walk, and the glow of a goddess! So truly divine that I immediately resolved to substitute myself for Fradique in the story, becoming the guide and floating along with immortals as they were towed along the river of immortality. She would be murmuring, faint with passion, alongside my face, not Fradique's, amidst the priestly granites of Medinet-Abu, the sweetest phrases from the *Anthology*! In a dream at least I was making a triumphal trip to Thebes. And I would make the subscribers to the *Gazeta de Portugal* think, "What a wonderful time he must have had there!"

Fradique sat down and received from Jove and the nymph, as they passed, a smile whose sweetness also took me in. I quickly pulled my chair closer to the poet of the *Inscriptions* and asked, "Who is that man? I know his face . . ."

"Of course, from pictures . . . That's Gautier!"

Gautier! Théophile Gautier! The great Théo! The flawless master and another rapture of my youth! I hadn't been mistaken completely, then. If he wasn't an Olympian, he was at least the last pagan, preserving in these times of abstract and gray intellectualism the true religion of line and color. And this intimacy of Fradique's with the author of *Mademoiselle de Maupin* and with the old paladin of *Hernani* made that countryman of mine all the more precious to me, as he gave our worn-out nation such an original luster. In order to find out if he wanted anisette or gin I affectionately stroked his sleeve. And I was taken with wild excitement at his wit as he clarified for me the mumbling of the black man from Seneh. What I had taken for an announcement of a divine presence had meant merely *c'est le deux*! Gautier was in room number two at the hotel. For the barbarian, the plastic master of Romanticism was nothing but—Number *Two*.

I then told him about my pagan fantasy, the story I was working on, the perfect days of passion that awaited him on the trip to Nubia. I even asked permission to dedicate "Jupiter's Last Campaign" to him. Fradique smiled, thanked me, and only wished (he confessed) that it were a reality, because a woman of more genuine beauty and more intense seduction couldn't be found then that water nymph, whose name was Jeanne Morlaix and who was a member of the Délassements-Comiques troupe. But to his misfortune the radiant creature was slavishly in love with a certain Sicard, a stockbroker, who had brought her to Cairo and who had gone off that evening to dine with some Greek bankers in the Chubra gardens . . .

"In any case," that most original man went on, "I shall never forget your enchanting intention, my dear countryman."

Descartes it was, I think, who, as he mocked Epicurean or atomist physics, spoke somewhere about the charms produced by the *atomes crochus*, curved atoms shaped like a clasp or a fishhook, which invisibly hook one heart to another to form resistant chains like the bronzes of Samothrace and forever connect and fuse two beings in a conquering constancy of fate that outlives life. Some kind of *nothing* brings on that fateful or providential entwining of atoms. Sometimes it is a look, as so disastrously happened to Romeo and Juliet in Verona; sometimes it is the urge of two children for the same fruit in a royal orchard, as in the classical friendship of Orestes and Pylades. So it was, according to this theory (as satisfactory as any other in affective psychology), that the splendid adventure of love I had so generously reserved for Fradique in "Jupiter's Last Campaign" would be the mysterious and unconscious cause, the *nothing*, that determined his first liking for me, which after six years had developed and solidified into intellectual intimacy.

Many times over the course of our social relations Fradique would refer with thanks to that *charming intention* of mine of entwining the arms of Jeanne Morlaix around his neck. Had he been captivated by the sinuous and poetic homage that I was paying his manly seductive qualities in that way? I don't know. But when we got up to go see the display of lights for Beiram, Fradique, in a new, open, warm, almost intimate way, began to use the familiar form of address with me.

The display of lights in the Orient, the same as that in Minho, consists of small cups of clay and glass in which a wick or a fuse of tow is burning. But the great profusion with which the little cups are spread about (when the Pasha pays for them) turns old decrepit cities, decorated like that in praise of Allah, into something truly dazzling, especially for a Westerner anointed with literature and inclined to see reproduced everywhere in the modern Orient the much-read wonders of those *Thousand and One Nights* that no one has ever read.

During the Beiram celebrations (paid for by the Khedive), the little cups were beyond count, and the whole outline of Cairo, even the meanest and most fugitive parts, stood out in the dark night, splendidly ennobled by lines of light. Long rows of shining dots marked out roof terraces, doors opened on hinges of light, a fringe of light sparkled from canopies, a glimmer trembled on every leaf on every tree from the breeze, and the minarets, which Oriental poetry has compared for centuries to the arms of the earth lifted up to heaven, shined like arms with gleaming bracelets in the serene shadows of that festive night. It was (as I mentioned to Fradique) as if all through the day a thick dusting of gold had fallen over the sordid city, settling onto the friezes and the grillwork of the Moorish balconies and now sparkling radiantly in the dark of the calm night.

But the unique and new beauty lay for me in that festive multitude crowding into squares and bazaars and which Fradique, over all the noise and dust, was explaining to me as he would have in a picture book. With such depth and detail did this admirable countryman of mine know the East! Of all those sharply diverse peoples, from their color or their clothing, he knew their race, their history, their customs, and their place in Muslim civilization. Slowly, buttoned up in a flannel jacket and with a kurbash whip (which in Egypt is the emblem of authority) tucked under his arm, he went about pointing out and naming for my eager curiosity the strange figures that I was comparing, laughing, to those of some fabulous masquerade put together by an archeologist, during a night of erudite fun, in an attempt to reproduce the "ways" of the Semites and their "types" down through the ages: here fellahs, laughing and agile in their long blue cotton robes; there solemn Bedouins, moving gravely, with their shins bound up in bandages and heavy scimitars in scarlet sheaths hanging from their chests; farther on were Abadiehs, with hair shaped in the form of haystacks and spiked with hedgehog quills that crowned them with black halos . . . Those on one side, with an insolent bearing, long mustaches that fluttered in the wind, and precious knives glowing in the silk belts of their short, puffy skirts, were the Argonauts from Macedonia; those over there, beautiful Greek sculptures carved out of ebony, were men from Senar; others, with heads wrapped in yellow cloths with broad fringes that looked like pilgrims' cowls embroidered in gold, were horsemen from Hejaz . . . And he went on pointing out and explaining so many others to me: unkempt Jews with curly ringlets, Copts who looked like senators in their togas, black soldiers from Darfur wearing linen fatigue jackets stained with dust and blood, ulemas in green turbans, Persians in felt miters, mosque beggars covered with scabs, Turkish scribes, pompous and fat, in gold-trimmed vests . . . What more can I say? A glittering carnival where, passing at every moment, shaken by the donkey's trot, on red pack saddles, were great puffy sacks—women. And all that noisy and magnificent crowd moved along with invocations to Allah and the beating of tambourines, with strident moans coming from the strings of the durbakas, and with slow songs, those Arab songs that had a voluptuousness so mournful and so harsh that Fradique said they pierced a person's soul with a "scraping caress." But here and there among the decrepit and lacelike houses a white façade would show, the wealthy house of a sheikh or a pasha, with an arched balcony through which there could be glimpsed inside, in the silence of a harem, silk hangings and gold embroidery, a tremor of light on the crystals of the chandeliers, slender shapes under their thin veils . . . Then the crowds would stop, fall quiet, and from all lips came a great *Ah!*, languid and amazed.

We were walking along like that when, coming out of the Mujik, Fradique Mendes stopped and quite gravely exchanged a salaam with a pale young man with gleaming eyes. It was that oriental greeting in which the fingers touch three times: forehead, mouth, and heart. And I laughed as I envied that intimacy he showed with "a man in a green robe and a Persian miter."

"He's an ulema from Baghdad," Fradique said, "of an ancient caste, of superior intelligence . . . One of the finest and most charming people I had met in Persia."

Then, with the familiarity that had been growing stronger between us, I asked Fradique what it was that had kept him in Persia for a whole year and a day, as they say in fairy tales. And Fradique, with complete simplicity, confessed that he had lingered so long on the banks of the Euphrates because he had become by chance involved with a religious movement, which since 1849 was enjoying an almost triumphal development in Persia and which was called Babism. Attracted by that new sect out of critical curiosity and in order to observe how a religion is born and founded, he had come, little by little, to have taken an active interest in Babism, not from any admiration for its doctrine, but from the veneration of its apostles. Babism (he told me as he led me into an alley that was more solitary and favorable for confidences) had as its initiator a certain Mirza Mohammad, one of those messiahs who turn up every day in the incessant religious ferment of the Orient, where religion is the supreme and beloved occupation of life. Familiar with the Christian Gospels through contact with missionaries, initiated in the pure Mosaic tradition by the Jews of Hiraz, with a profound knowledge of Ghebrism, the old national religion of Persia, Mirza Mohammad brought these doctrines together with a purer and more abstract conception of Islam and declared himself to be Bab. In Persian, *Bab* means "door." He was, then, *the door*, the only door through which men could ever enter into the absolute Truth. More literally, Mirza Mohammad presented himself as the great doorkeeper, the man chosen from among all by the Lord to open the door of Truth to all believers and, therefore, that of Paradise. In short, he was a Messiah, a Christ. As such he went through the classic evolution of messiahs: as his first disciples he had the shepherds and women of an obscure village; he suffered his temptations on the mountain; he fulfilled his expiating penances; he preached in parables; in Mecca he scandalized the doctors; and he suffered his passion, dying either (I can't remember which) beheaded or shot after the feast of Ramadan in Tabriz.

"Well," Fradique went on, "in the Muslim world there are two religious divisions, the Shia and the Sunni. The Persians are Shias while the Turks are Sunnis. These differences, however, basically have a more political and racial character than a theological or dogmatic one, even though a fellah from the Nile will always despise a Persian from the Euphrates as a *foul heretic*. The discord reappears, stronger and more fearsome, whenever Shias or Sunnis need to take a stand in the face of a new interpretation of doctrine or the new appearance of a prophet. Therefore, Babism among the Shias ran up against a hostility that grew to the point of persecution, and that, of course, meant that it would be received with deference and sympathy by the Sunnis."

On the basis of that Fradique, who had forged a familiar relationship in

Baghdad with one of the most vigorous and authoritative apostles of Babism, Said El-Suriz (whose son he had saved from swamp fever by an application of fruit salt), and while they were chatting on his roof terrace one day about those lofty spiritual interests, had suggested to him the idea of supporting Babism among the agricultural peoples of the Nile and the nomadic peoples of Libya. Among men of the Sunni sect Babism would find an easy field for conversions, and it is the traditional route of sectarian movements in the East, as everywhere, that they rise up from the sincere popular masses before they reach the cultured classes. Perhaps that new wave of religious emotion could manage to penetrate education in some of the mosques in Cairo, especially the El-Azhar mosque, the great university of the East, where the younger ulemas make up a cohort of enthusiasts, always disposed toward innovations and apostolates of combatants. By winning theological advantage there and acquiring a literary polish, Babism could then have an advantage in attacking the old fortresses of dogmatic Islam. This idea made a deep impression on Said El-Suriz. That pale young man with whom Fradique had exchanged the salaam had been sent out immediately as a Babist emissary to Medina-Abu (the ancient Thebes) to sound out Sheikh Ali-Hussein, a man of decisive influence in the whole valley of the Nile for his knowledge and virtue. And he, Fradique, having no pressing business in the West at the moment and full of curiosity about that picturesque Advent, was also leaving for Thebes, planning to meet the Babist on the Nile in Beni-Sueff at the waning of the moon . . .

After so many years I can't remember whether this was how things really were but I do know that the way Fradique revealed them as we strolled through the festivities in Cairo had won me over completely. While he was going on about the Bab, that apostolic mission to the old sheikh in Thebes, another faith rising up in the Muslim world with its cortège of martyrs and ecstasies, and the possible establishment of a new Babist empire, the man began taking on proportions of grandeur in my eyes. I had never known anyone involved in such lofty matters and, at the same time, I felt both proud and terrified at receiving this sublime secret. My emotion would have been no different if on the eve of Saint Paul's sailing for Greece, carrying the Word to the Gentiles, I had strolled with him through the narrow streets of Seleucia listening to his hopes and dreams!

Chatting like that we entered the plaza of the El-Azhar mosque, where the celebration for the feast of Beiram was even more noisy and tumultuous. But I wasn't caught up in the surprises of that Muslim festival, neither Indian dancers swirling around with flashes of red and gold, nor desert poets reciting the deeds of Antar, nor dervishes in their linen canopies wailing in rhythm their praises of Allah . . . Silent, I had been taken over by thoughts of the Bab, turning over in my mind a confused desire to become involved in that spiritual campaign. What if I went to Thebes with Fradique? . . . Why not? I had the youth, I had the enthusiasm. It would be more virile and noble to take up the career of an evangelist in the East than to banally resume in banal Lisbon my scribbling on a pad under the gas lights of the *Gazeta de Portugal.* And little by little out of this desire, just the same as from boiling water, the slow vapor of a vision was rising up. I was seeing myself as a disciple of the Bab, receiving that night from the Baghdad ulema initiation into the Truth. And I was leaving at once to preach and spread the Babist word. Where would I go? To Portugal, of course, bearing salvation for the souls dearest to me. Like Saint Paul I would embark on a galley, with storms attacking my apostolic bow. The image of the Bab appeared to me over the waters and his serene gaze filled my soul with unconquerable strength. One day I finally caught sight of land and in the clear morning I was cutting through the clear waters of the Tagus, where for so many centuries no envoy of God had entered. Then from a distance I cursed the churches of Lisbon, buildings of a worn-out and less pure faith. I disembarked, leaving my belongings behind in a new attitude of divine detachment from old worldly goods, and I bounded along that blessed Rua do Alecrim. In the middle of Loreto, just when the Director-Generals were climbing up slowly from the Arcade, I opened my arms and roared, "I am the Door!"

I didn't plunge into the Babist apostolate, but it so happened that, carried away by those fantasies, I had lost Fradique and I didn't know the way back to the Shepheard's Hotel, nor in order to find out did I have any words in Arabic except those for *water* and *love*! Those were anxious moments in which, stupefied, I sniffed my way through the El-Azhar square, stumbling into fires where coffee was brewing, colliding inconsiderately with rude armed Bedouins. Then, by the time when I was already shouting out Fradique's name over the crowd, I ran into him placidly contemplating an Indian dancer . . .

But he went right along, with a shrug of his shoulders. Nor did he allow me, up ahead, to stop and admire a poet who, in the midst of astounded fellahs and Maghrebins leaning on their lances, was reading in a languorous and sad tone from a few greasy sheets of paper. Dance and poetry, Fradique stated, the two great arts of the Orient, were in a miserable state of decadence. Both had lost their tradition of pure style. Dancers had been perverted by the influence of the casinos of Ezbekieh, where they strutted the can-can, and were now polluting the grace of the old Arab dances, throwing a leg up into the air in the vile manner of Marseilles fashion. And the same banality, along with extravagance, was triumphing in poetry. The delicate forms of Persian classicism weren't followed and were practically unknown. The fountain of imagination has run dry among Muslims and poor Oriental poetry, which had once treated age-old themes with a delicate stress, has, like ours, fallen into a barbarous Parnassianism . . .

"So," I said softly, "the East . . ."

"Is just as mediocre as the West."

And we slowly returned to the hotel as Fradique, finishing his cigar, told me that the Oriental spirit today lives only in philosophical activity stirred up every morning by some new and complicated concept of morality offered it by bazaar logicians and desert metaphysicians.

The next day I went with Fradique to Bulak, where he would embark for Upper Egypt. His *debarieh* was waiting, tied to its mooring stake close to the houses of old Cairo and among boats from Aswan loaded with lentils and sweet cane. The sun was sinking into the Libyan sands and up above the sky was going to sleep, without a shadow, without a cloud, pure throughout like the soul of the just. A file of Coptic women with yellow jugs on their shoulders was coming down singing to the waters of the Nile, blessed among all waters. And the ibises, before they settled in their nests, were arriving, just as they did in times when they were gods, to cast their twilight blessing over the housetops with a flap of their contented wings.

I went along behind Fradique into the glass-enclosed saloon of the *debarieh*, where weapons were hanging for morning hunts and books lay for siesta and study in the calm, when the boat goes slowly along behind the tow rope. Then for a few moments on deck we silently contemplated those banks, which over the ages had brought on the enchantment for all who had been there and felt, like us, that along them life is full of a greater good and a supreme sweetness. How many others, since the rude shepherds who demolished Tanis, have lingered here like us surveying these waters, these skies, with greedy, ecstatic, or nostalgic eyes: Kings of Judah, Kings of Assyria, Kings of Persia; the magnificent Ptolemies; Prefects of Rome and Prefects of Byzantium; Amru, sent by Mohammed, and Saint Louis sent by Christ; Alexander the Great, dreaming of his eastern empire; Bonaparte, picking up that immense dream; and also those who only came to tell about this adorable land, from the loquacious Herodotus to the first of the Romantics, the pale man with his great *pose* who spoke of the sorrows of *René*![7] This divine and unequalled landscape is quite well known. The Nile flows on, paternal and fecund. Farther along it is green, where under the flight of doves lie the gardens and orchards of Rhoda. Farther still, the palm trees of Giza, delicate and bronze-like in the golden light of afternoon, shelter villages that have the simplicity of nests. At the edge of the desert, rising up in the pride of their eternity, are the three pyramids. With that alone, a person's soul remains here fixed in memory, but in order to live in this soft beauty peoples have waged long wars on each other.

But the time had come. I embraced Fradique with singular emotion. The sail was unfurled to the soft breeze that rippled through the mimosa leaves. On the bow, the master lifted his arms, palms up to Heaven, and called out, "In the name of Allah, the kind and merciful, who carries us along!" All around, from other boats, slow voices murmur, "In the name of Allah, may he carry you!" One of the oarsmen, sitting on a gunwale, struck his darbuka while another picked up a clay flute. And in the midst of blessings and songs, the wide boat cut through the sacred waters, carrying my incomparable friend to Thebes.

IV

It was years before I ran into Fradique Mendes again, as he was taken up traveling in western Europe while I was wandering about America, the Antilles, and the republics around the Gulf of Mexico. When my life finally settled down in an old rural part of England, Fradique was involved once more in the "ethnographic scheme" he mentions in a letter to Oliveira Martins and was beginning his long trip to Brazil, the pampas, Chile, and Patagonia.

But the thread of congeniality that had joined us together in Cairo hadn't broken, nor had we, in spite of its being so tenuous, allowed it to be lost among the more pressing interests of our divergent fortune. We would exchange letters almost every three months—five or six pages in which I would accumulate a tumult of images and impressions and which Fradique would fill, in great detail, with ideas and facts. In addition to this, I would find out about Fradique through some of my old friends with whom, during a more intimate stay of his in Lisbon lasting from October of 1875 to the summer of 1876, he had established friendships in which they all found intellectual profit and charm.

All of them, in spite of being unlike in temperament and having different outlooks on life, had, the same as I, fallen under the charm of that enchanting man. In November of 1877, the author of *Contemporary Portugal*[8] wrote me, "I have just met your Fradique, whom I consider to be the most interesting Portuguese person of the nineteenth century. He bears a curious resemblance to

Descartes! It's that same passion for travel, which would bring the philosopher to close his books 'in order to study the great book of the world,' the same attraction for luxury and commotion, which in Descartes was translated into the pleasure of frequenting courts and armies, the same love of mystery and sudden disappearances, the same vanity, never confessed but intense, of birth and nobility, the same calm courage, the same singular mixture of romantic instincts and precise reason, of fantasy and geometry. With all of this, he still lacks any serious or supreme goal in life that these qualities, so excellent in themselves, might combine to bring about. And I suspect that instead of a *Discourse on Method* he will end up leaving nothing but a vaudeville show." Ramalho Ortigão later said of him in a warm letter, "Fradique Mendes is the most complete, the most finished product of civilization that my eyes have been given to drink in. No one is better equipped for triumph in art and in life. The rose in his lapel is always of the freshest, just as the idea in his spirit is always of the most original. He can hike along for five leagues without a stop, defeat the best oarsmen of Oxford, go alone into the jungle to hunt tigers, charge a body of Abyssinian lancers with only a whip in his hand, and at night, in a salon, wearing his dinner jacket from Cook's with a black pearl gleaming in the splendor of his shirt front, he will smile at the ladies with the same charm and aplomb with which he smiled in the face of fatigue, danger, and death. He fences like the Chevalier de Saint-Georges and he holds the newest and most certain notions in physics, astronomy, philology, and metaphysics. He is a model, a lesson in good taste. Just look at him in his rooms, in his private life of a gentleman traveler, among his Russian-leather suitcases, his broad brushes with silverwork, his silk tunics, his Winchester rifles, preparing himself and choosing a scent, sipping some tea sent him by the Grand Duke Vladimir, and dictating to a servant in knee breeches, more venerably correct than a majordomo of Louis XIV, telegrams that will carry news of him to boudoirs in Paris and London. And after all this, he closes his door to the world and sits down to read Sophocles in the original."

The poet of *The Death of Don Juan* and *The Muse on Vacation* called him "a Saint-Beuve bound in Alcides."[9] And this is how, in a letter I still have from those days, he described Fradique's appearance in the world: "One day God took a pinch of Heinrich Heine, another of Chateaubriand, a third one of Brummel, some fiery bits of Renaissance adventurers, dried fragments of scholars of the Institut de France, poured champagne and printer's ink over it and kneaded it all with His omnipotent hands, quickly shaping Fradique and tossing him down to Earth, saying, 'Go get yourself outfitted at Poole's!'" Lastly, Carlos Meyer, lamenting like Oliveira Martins that Fradique's multiple and strong aptitudes lacked coordination and a convergence toward any higher goal, one day gave a wise, deep summary of my friend's personality: "Fradique's brain is admirably constructed and furnished. All it lacks is for an idea to take up residence in it, to live and to govern inside there. Fradique is a genius with some writings!"

Also, that same winter, Fradique met the thinker of the *Modern Odes*, of whom, in one of his letters to Oliveira Martins, he speaks with such distinction and warmth.[10] And the last companion of my youth to meet the onetime poet of the *Inscriptions* was J. Texeira de Azevedo, in the summer of 1877 in Sintra, at the Saragoça estate where Fradique had come to rest up from his trip to Brazil and republics of the Pacific Coast. They chatted for a long time and always disagreed. J. Teixeira de Azevedo, being a nervous and passionate person, felt an overwhelming antipathy for what he called Fradique's *lymphatic criticism*. A man who was all emotion could not blend intellectually with that man who was all analysis. Nor did Fradique's extensive knowledge impress him. "The notions of that erudite dandy," he wrote in 1879, "are chunks of the *Larousse* diluted with eau-de-cologne." And, finally, certain affectations of Fradique's (silver-handled brushes and silk shirts), his sharp voice which cut out words with perfection and preciosity, his habit of drinking champagne with soda, and other traits still brought on an almost physical irritation in my old comrade from the Travessa do Guarda-Mor. He confessed, however, like Oliveira Martins, that Fradique was the most interesting and suggestive Portuguese person of the nineteenth century. He corresponded with him regularly, but in order to contradict him acrimoniously.

In 1880 (nine years after my wanderings in the Orient), I was spending Easter week in Paris. One night after the opera, I went to dine alone at the Bignon. I had started on my oysters and a column in *Le Temps*, when, from behind the newspaper, which I had rested against the wine bottle, a broad, glowing mass appeared. It consisted of a vest, a dress shirt, a cravat, and a face, all of an incomparable whiteness. A very calm voice said softly, "We left each other on the docks at Bulak . . ." I arose with a shout. Fradique was smiling and the maître d'hôtel drew back, startled by the Southern and noisy effusion of my embrace. Our intellectual intimacy really dated from that night in Paris, and for eight years it has always been the same and always secure, with no intermission or shadows to cloud its purity.

I must call it *intellectual* because that intimacy never went beyond matters of the mind. In the happy times I shared with him in Paris, London, and Lisbon from 1880 to 1887, I was always intimate and without reserve, in our copious correspondence, with Fradique's intelligence and I took part in and mingled with his thinking life without interruption, but I never penetrated his affectionate side of sentiment and heart. Nor, in truth, was I tormented by any curiosity to know it, perhaps because I felt that Fradique's rare originality was completely concentrated in his thinking self and that his other self, the sensual one, made of ordinary clay, would repeat with no special distinction the usual weakness of clay. Furthermore, from that Easter night in Paris when our relationship began, we always followed the special habit, a bit proud and strict perhaps, of thinking of ourselves as two pure spirits. If I had then conceived an original philosophy or prepared the commandments of a new religion, or pilfered from a distracted Nature one of her secret laws, out of preference I would have chosen Fradique as the confidante for that mental activity, but never would I go to him in matters of sentiment with the secret of a hope or a disappointment. And Fradique, likewise, maintained this attitude of inaccessible reserve with me, never showing himself to my eyes except in his intellectual function.

I well remember one splendid May morning when we were going along chatting through the Tuileries Gardens, underneath the flowering chestnut trees. Fradique, who was resting his arm on mine, was slowly developing the idea that the extreme democratization of science, its universal and unlimited spread among the people, was the greatest mistake of our civilization, because with this it was speedily laying the ground for its moral catastrophe . . . Suddenly, as we were passing through the gate to the Place de la Concorde, the philosopher, who was casting his predictions of a final disaster in the midst of all that tender May greenery, stopped and fell silent. Before us, sprightly passing by to the dainty pace of a fine mare toward the rue Royale, was a coupé, in which I caught a shadowy glimpse of the satin lining and a head of honey-colored hair. Sprightly too, Fradique shook my hand, babbled a "Goodbye!," called to a fiacre, and disappeared behind the gallop of its nag in the direction of the Quai d'Orsay. "A woman!" I thought. It was, in fact, the woman who had been his torment, as he reported in a letter to Madame de Jouarre, dated "May, Saturday," and beginning, "Yesterday, as I was philosophizing with a friend in the Tuileries Gardens . . ." In that fiacre, Fradique was chasing after a most rude and mortifying disappointment. Later that afternoon at dusk, I went as planned to pick Fradique up on the rue de Varennes, at the old Tredennes palace, where he had been staying since Christmas in rooms furnished in a luxury that was quite noble and sober. No sooner had I entered the parlor that we had named the "heroic room," because it was dressed up with four tapestries by Lucas Cornelisz that told the story of "The Labors of Hercules," than Fradique left the window where he had been looking out at the park, which was already mingled with the shadows, and came calmly over to me, his hands buried in the pockets of a silk smoking jacket. And, as if from that morning on there had been no other care to absorb him except our theme in the Tuileries Garden, he continued:

"I didn't get to tell you a while back . . . Science, my dear fellow, must be withdrawn into sanctuaries, as in times past. There is no other way of saving ourselves from moral anarchy. It must be withdrawn into sanctuaries and turned over to a sacred intellectual college, which will guard it and defend it against the curiosity of the common people . . . A program must be set up for coming generations with this idea in mind."

Had I noticed, I might have spotted on his face some remnants of pallor and emotion, but his tone was simple and firm, that of a critic genuinely occupied in the deduction of his conceit. Any other man who had gone through such a mortifying and cruel disappointment a few hours before would have at least muttered in a general and impersonal way, "Ah, my friend, how stupid is life!"; but he spoke of science and the common people, determinedly laying out before me, or imposing on himself perhaps, the reasoning of his brain, so that my eyes wouldn't penetrate even slightly or so that his mind wouldn't linger too long on the bitterness he held in his heart.

In a letter to Oliveira Martins in 1883, Fradique says, "Man, like the ancient kings of the Orient, must not show anything of himself to his fellows except his being solely and calmly *occupied in the business of ruling, that is, of thinking.*" This rule, which came from a pride permissible only in a Spinoza or a Kant, firmly governed his conduct. That was how he invariably behaved with me, at least, during our active companionship, never opening up or offering himself fully, except in matters of the intellect. For that reason perhaps, more than any other man, he exerted domination over me and held an attraction for me.

V

What was immediately impressive about Fradique's intelligence or, rather, about his way of using it was the supreme freedom he took, along with a supreme audacity. I never knew any other spirit so impermeable to tyranny or the infiltration of "accepted ideas," and surely no other man ever translated his original and very own thinking with more calm and proud self-possession. "In spite of thirty centuries of geometry telling me (he says in a letter to J. Teixeira de Azevedo) that *a straight line is the shortest distance between two points*, if I were to find out that it was more direct and quicker for me to get from the door of the Hotel Universal to the door of the Casa Havanesa by going round through the Bairro de São Martinho and the heights of Graça, I would declare, therefore, that the shortest distance between two points is a crazy, wandering *curve*." This independence from Reason, which Fradique preached in such a disorderly fantasy, constituted a rare quality; but his manner of stating it so fearlessly before the majesty of tradition and rule or the oracular conclusions of the Masters is truly a virtue, and a most rare one, a brilliantly exceptional one.

In another letter to J. Teixeira de Azevedo, Fradique speaks of a Polish professor and critic named G. Cornuski, who wrote in the *Swiss Review* and who (Fradique says) "constantly took a very great pleasure and a very personal one in rebelling against works of literature and art which critical consensus over the centuries has consecrated as masterpieces—Tasso's *Gerusalemme Liberata*, Titian's canvases, the tragedies of Racine, Bossuet's orations, our own *Lusiads*, and other canonized monuments. But whenever his integrity as a professor and critic imposed the proclamation of truth on him, this robust and full-blooded man who had fought heroically in two insurrections, would tremble and think: 'No! Why is my criterion more secure than that of such shrewd bits of understanding that have come down through the ages? Who knows, perhaps there is something sublime in those works and in my spirit there is an impotence for understanding it?' And poor Cornuski, his soul sadder than an autumn sunset, would go on listening to the choruses of *Atalia* and looking at Titian's nudes and muttering disconsolately 'How beautiful!'

"Rare are those who suffer the critical anguish of poor Cornuski. All, however, with pleasant unawareness, keep on practicing their intellectual servility. As a matter of fact, either because our spirits do not have the manly courage to face up to the authority of those to whom the sturdiest criterion and high knowledge is traditionally attributed; or because established ideas, floating about diffusely in our memories after readings and conversations appear to us to be our own; or because the suggestion of those conceits imposes itself on us and leads us subtly to end up agreeing with them—the lamentable truth is that all of us today tend slavishly to think and feel the way people before us and around us have already felt and thought."

"Nineteenth-century man, the European, because only he essentially exists in the nineteenth century (Fradique states in a letter to Carlos Mayer), lives inside a pale, insipid *infection of banality*, brought on by the forty thousand volumes that England, France and Germany pile up every year, sweating and groaning, on street corners, and in which they endlessly and monotonously reproduce, with an occasional touch of make-up applied, the four ideas and the four impressions handed down by Antiquity and the Renaissance. The state channels this infection through its schools. This, my dear Carolus, is what they call *education*! The child, starting with his first primer, while still barely able to spell, begins to absorb this layer of the commonplace, a layer that later on, for every day of his life, newspapers, magazines, pamphlets, and books will keep packing into his spirit, turning it as useless for production as soil whose native fertility has died under the sand and gravel barbarously raked into it. In order for a European to attain any new ideas of flourishing originality today he would have to isolate himself in the desert or on the pampas and there wait patiently for nature's living breath to penetrate his intelligence, slowly sweeping it clean of the detritus of twenty centuries of literature and restoring its virginity. Therefore I maintain, oh, Carolus Mayerensis, that an intelligence that proudly wishes to acquire the divine power of generation must go cure itself of literary civilization with the tonic of a two-year residence among the Hottentots or the Patagonians. Patagonia works on the intellect the way Vichy water works on the liver, clearing away obstructions and allowing it the healthy exercise of its natural function. After two years of a savage life among the naked Hottentots, moving about in the thoroughgoing logic of instinct, what will remain for a civilized man of all his ideas of progress, morality, religion, industry, political economy, literature, and art? Tatters. The hanging tatters of the trousers and jacket he had brought from Europe after twenty months of jungle and swamp. And not having any books or magazines around to renew his store of 'accepted ideas,' or any useful Nunes Algibebe to supply him with a ready-to-wear suit, the European will return without realizing it to the nobility of the primitive state: nudity of the body and originality of the soul. When he returns, he will be an Adam, strong and pure, virginal of any literature, with his skull clean of all the conceits and notions that have been piling up since Aristotle, able to proceed superbly in a completely new examination of human matters. I ask you, Carlos, spirit who distills *spirits*, would you care to plunge back with me into the Origins and come with me to the inspiring land of the Hottentots? There, free and naked, stretched out in the sun between the palm grove and the stream, which will give protective sustenance to our bodies, with our strong lance stuck into the turf and women beside us pouring out over us the portion of poetry and dreams that the soul needs, we will free our sides to burst into laughter at the idea of great philosophies, great moralities, great economics, and great criticism, and all the great rascalities that roam all over this Europe, where thick and high-hatted herds keep bumping into each other, stupefied by the superstitions of civilization, by

the illusion of gold, by the pedantry of science, by the mystifications of reform-
ers, by the slavery of routine, and by the stupid admiration of themselves! . . ."

Thus spoke Fradique. This "completely new examination of human matters," however, possible, according to the poet of the *Inscriptions*, for the renovated Adam who has returned from Patagonia, his spirit cleansed of the dust
and garbage of long years of literature, he attempted to find without leaving his
classical walls on the rue de Varennes, with incomparable vigor and sincerity.
And in this he showed moral intrepidness. His tastes and habits irresistibly held
him in the world, a temperate and mediocre world without any invention or
intellectual initiative, where ideas, in order to be pleasing, must follow "univer-
sally accepted" manners and not those created with individuality. In this world
Fradique, free with his brusque and restless judgments, was in danger of being
taken for a petulant seeker of originality, avid for small glory and standing out
too much. An inventive and new spirit with a strength for thinking very much
in his own way, who lets the abundant and multiple life that drives and fills him
overflow, is more disagreeable to this world than the rudely natural man who
doesn't regulate and keep within the bounds of "social rules" the length of his
hair, the stridency of his guffaws, and the free movement of his sturdy limbs.
About this undisciplined and creative spirit come immediate mutterings of dis-
trust, "Pretentious! Looking for attention and effect." And Fradique hated nothing more intensely than *excessive attention* and *effect*. I never saw him wear
anything but dark neckwear. And he would prefer anything over being pointed
out as one of those men who, albeit bearing no deep dislike for Diana and her
cult, and with the sole purpose of being spoken about with awe in the streets,
head out during festivities brandishing a great torch in order to set fire to her
temple in Ephesus. He would prefer anything except (as he says in a letter to
Madame de Jouarre) "having to dress Truth from the warehouses of the Louvre
in order to be able to enter in her company the house of Anne de Varle, Duchess
of Varle and Orgemont. To enter, I should escort my friend naked, completely
naked, treading on the tapestries with her naked feet, thrusting at the men the
fecund tips of her noble, naked breasts. *Amicus mundus, sed magis amica Veritas*!
That beautiful Latin means, my godmother, that I basically judge originality to
be pleasing to women and only disagreeable to men, which leads me to love it
twice as stubbornly."

This independence, this free elasticity of spirit and intense sincerity—which
prevented him from being seduced into giving himself over completely to any
System, where he would remain forever through inertia—were, furthermore, the
qualities that best fitted the type of intellectual function that had become for

Fradique the most continuous and the most preferred. "Unfortunately (he wrote to Oliveira Martins in 1882), there is neither a sage nor a philosopher in me. I mean that I am not one of those secure and useful men destined by temperament for that secondary analysis called Science, which consists in the reduction of a multitude of scattered facts to particular types and laws that explain the modalities of the universe. Nor am I one of those fascinating and not too secure men destined by genius to the superior analysis called Philosophy, which consists of reducing those laws and those types to a general formula that explains the very essence of the entire Universe. Not being, therefore, either a sage or a philosopher, I cannot contribute to the betterment of my kind either by increasing their well-being by means of science, which is a producer of wealth, or by uplifting their feeling of contentment by means of metaphysics, which is an inspirer of poetry. Entry into History also continues to be denied me, for in order to produce literature all that is needed is to possess talent, but to attempt history it is best to possess virtues. And as for me! Therefore, all that is left for me is to be, by way of ideas and facts, a man who passes through, infinitely curious and observant. The selfish occupation of my spirit today, my dear historian, consists of my approaching an idea or a fact and slipping smoothly into it, covering its every detail, exploring all there is of the unknown in it, enjoying all the intellectual surprises and emotions it can give, carefully collecting the lesson or the parcel of truth that exists in its folds, and leaving it to go on to another fact, or idea, leisurely and peacefully, as one passes through, one by one, the cities of a country where there is art and luxury. That's the way I visited Italy a while back, carried away by its colors and forms. Temporally and spiritually I have become nothing but a tourist."

Such tourists of the intelligence abound in France and England, but Fradique didn't limit himself, like them, to superficial and impersonal examinations, the way someone in an Oriental city will retain the notions and tastes of a European, studying only the visible relief of the monuments and the clothing of the crowds. Fradique (to continue his image) would transform himself into a "citizen of the cities he was visiting." He maintained as a principle that it was momentarily necessary to *believe* in order to understand a belief well. In that way he made himself a Babist in order to penetrate and reveal Babism. In that way, in Paris, he joined a revolutionary club called The Panthers of Batignolles and attended their meetings wearing a filthy jacket that was held together with pins, in hopes of plucking there "the flower of some instructive extravagance." In that way, in London, he joined in the Positivist rituals, where during feast days on the Comtist calendar they go about burning incense and myrrh on the altar of

Humanity and decorating the image of Auguste Comte with roses. In like manner he joined the Theosophists, contributed generously to the founding of *The Spiritist Review*, and presided over the Evocations on the rue Cardinet wearing a linen tunic and standing between the two superior mediums, Patoff and Lady Thorgan. In the same way he lived for a long summer in Seo de Urgel, the Catholic citadel of Carlism, "in order to disentangle properly (he said) what the motives and formulas are that go to make up a Carlist, because all things sectarian obey the reality of a motive and the illusion of a formula." In that way he became the confidante of the venerable Prince Kobalskini, "in order to be able to dismantle and study, piece by piece, the mechanism of the brain of a nihilist." In that same way he was preparing (when death took him by surprise) to return to India to become a practicing Buddhist, in order to make a thorough penetration of Buddhism, on which he had been focusing his curiosity and critical activity in his last years. So it might be said of him that he was a devotee of all religions, a partisan of all parties, a disciple of all philosophies, a comet wandering through ideas and absorbing with conviction from each and every one an increase in substance, but leaving in each something of the heat and energy of the movement of his thought. Those who know him imperfectly classified Fradique as a dilettante. No! There was a conviction (which the English call earnestness) in the way Fradique threw himself into the true basis of things, which gave his life a value and a power quite superior to those imparted by dilettantism, the skeptical diversion that drew so many insults from Carlyle, to natures that let themselves drop delightfully into it. The dilettante really just skims along over ideas and facts the way butterflies (to whom he has long been compared over the ages) flit among flowers, alighting and immediately picking up their lighthearted flight again, finding supreme delight in that mutability. Fradique, however, would go along like the bee, patiently extracting the honey from each plant. What I mean is that he went along gathering that "parcel of truth" that each one invariably contains, as man after man has nurtured it with interest and with passion.

That is how his high and diligent intelligence worked. But what was its essential and intrinsic quality? As far as I could see, Fradique's supreme intellectual quality always seemed to be an extraordinary perception of reality. "Every phenomenon (he says in a letter to Antero de Quental, suggestive through the obscurity that enwraps it) contains a reality. The expression *reality* is not philosophical, but I use it and toss it out, feeling around in it in order to pick up from inside the most possible part of a barely coercible concept, one that is almost irreducible to being put into words. Every phenomenon, therefore, as it exists in relation to our understanding and the latter's power of discrimination, has a reality, by which I mean certain characteristics, or (to express myself with an image, as Buffon recommends) certain *contours* that limit it, define it, give it its own makeup in the scattered and universal complex and constitute its *exact, real,* and *unique* mode of being. Only ignorance, error, prejudice, tradition, routine, and, above all, *illusion* will form around every phenomenon a fog that shades and deforms its contours and prevents intellectual vision from making out its *exact, real,* and *unique* mode of being. It is precisely what happens to monuments in London, sunk in the fog . . . This all comes out expressed in a most hesitant and incomplete way! Outside the sun is beaming down from a fine, clear sky on my convent yard covered with thick snow. In this so pure and clear atmosphere, where things take on a firm relief, I have lost all the flexibility and fluidity of philosophical technology. I could only express myself with images clipped out with shears. But you must certainly understand, excellent and subtle Antero. Have you ever been in London in the fall, in November? During a foggy morning on a London street, when it is difficult to tell whether the thick shadow taking shape in the distance is the statue of a hero or piece of wall, an ash-gray illusion submerges the whole city and a person who thought he was going into a church is amazed to find that he has entered a tavern. Just like that, for most human spirits, a similar fog is floating over the realities of life and the world. Out of this comes the fact that almost all of their steps are deviations, almost all of their judgments are deceptions, and these are constantly mixing up church and tavern. Rare are the intellectual visions that are sharp and powerful enough to break through the mist and come up with exact lines, the true contours of reality. There you have what I have been trying to stammer my way through."

There we have it! Fradique had at his disposal one of those privileged visions. The very way he had of slowly resting his eyes and *detailing things silently,* as Oliveira Martins used to say, immediately revealed his inner process of concentrating and applying reason, like a long and piercing arrow of light, until, the fog dispelled, reality would appear little by little in its rigorous and *unique* shape.

The most impressive manifestation of this magnificent force was his power to *define.* Possessing a spirit that *saw* with a maximum of exactitude, using a way of expression that *translated* things with a maximum of concision, made him capable of rendering absolutely profound and perfect summaries. I remember that one night at his place on the rue de Varennes in Paris there was a heated discussion about the nature of art. All the definitions of art proffered from Plato on down were repeated, along with others that were invented, where, as always, the phenomenon was seen in a limited way through a temperament. Fradique remained silent for some time, his eyes piercing empty space. Finally, in that slow way (which seemed professorial to those who knew him incompletely), spoken softly in the deferential silence that had grown longer, he said, "Art is a summary of nature done by the imagination."

I certainly do not know of a more complete definition of Art! And a friend of ours, a man with excellent powers of imagination, rightly affirmed that "if the good Lord, pitying our hesitations one day, were to toss down to us from his divine hermitage the final explanation of art, we would hear Fradique's definition resounding among the clouds, as superb as the rolling din of a hundred chariots of war."

Fradique's superior intelligence was supported by a strong and rich culture. His tools for knowledge were already considerable. In addition to a solid knowledge of the classical languages (which, during his age of poetry and decorative literature, had facilitated the creation of little poems in irregular Latin, like his beautiful "Laus Veneris Tenebrosae"), he possessed a thoroughgoing knowledge of the tongues of the three great thinking nations: France, England, and Germany. He also knew Arabic, and from what I was told by Riazz-Effendi, Sultan Abdulaziz's chronicler, he spoke it with breadth and good taste. •

The natural sciences were beloved and familiar to him and an insatiable and religious curiosity about the universe impelled him to study what divinely constitutes it, from insects to stars. These were studies made lovingly and with his heart because Fradique felt for nature, especially animal and plant life, a tenderness and veneration that were truly Buddhist. "I love nature for itself (he wrote me in 1882), in its totality and its individuality, in the grace and ugliness of each one of the innumerable forms that fill it. I love it too as a tangible and multiple manifestation of the supreme Unity, of the intangible Reality to which every religion and every philosophy gives a different name and to which I give my worship under the name of Life. In short, I worship Life, of which a rose and a scab are equal expressions, a constellation and (I confess with horror) Counselor Acácio.[11] I worship Life and therefore I worship everything, because everything is a form of living, even dying. A rigid corpse in its coffin is just as much alive as an eagle furiously flapping his wings as he takes flight. And my religion can all be in the credo of Athanasius, with a small variation: I believe in Almighty *Life*, the creator of Heaven and Earth . . ."

When our close friendship began in 1880, however, his restless spirit had been preferentially delving into the social sciences, especially those belonging to pre-history: anthropology, linguistics, the study of races, myths, and primitive institutions. Almost every three months, tall stacks of books sent from the house

of Hachette and thick layers of specialized journals scattered over his Caraman-
ian carpet indicated to me that some new curiosity was taking hold of him with
intensity and passion. I knew him to be successively and ardently occupied in
that way with the megalithic monuments of Andalusia, lake dwellings, the
mythology of the Aryan peoples, Chaldean magic, Polynesian races, the laws
and customs of the Kaffirs, the Christianization of the pagan gods . . . These
intense investigations lasted as long as he was able to extract from them some
"emotion or intellectual surprise." Then books and journals would disappear
one day and Fradique would triumphantly announce, "I've drunk up Sabaism
completely!" or "I've drained Polynesians down to the dregs!"

The study that held him without interruption, however, and with a special
constancy was that of history. "Ever since I was a child (he wrote to Oliveira
Martins in 1886 in one of his last letters), I've had a passion for history. And
can you guess why, Mr. Historian? For the comforting and intimate feeling that
it gives me of human solidarity. When I was eleven years old, my grandmother,
in order to get me used to the harsh things in life (as she put it), suddenly pulled
me out of Father Nunes's easy-going teaching and sent me to a school called
the Terceirense. The gardener would take me by the hand and every day Grandmother would solemnly give me a copper with which to buy a piece of cake for
lunch at Tia Marta's pastry shop on the corner. That servant, that copper, those
buns were new customs that wounded my monumental pride as the first-born
of an estate, having lowered me to the same humble level as the sons of our attorney. One day however, thumbing through an *Encyclopedia of Roman Antiquities*, which was illustrated, I read with surprise that boys in Rome (in grand
Rome!) also went to school in the morning like me, holding a hand of a slave
called the *capsarius*, and that they would buy a bun at some Tia Marta's in the
Velabrus or the Carinas to eat for lunch, which they called the *ientaculum*. So,
my dear fellow, at that very instant the venerable antiquity of those customs
took away from me everything about them that had given me so much humiliation. After having detested them because they were practiced by the sons of
Silva the lawyer, I respected them because they had been followed by the sons
of Scipio. The purchase of the bun became a kind of ritual, which ever since
antiquity all schoolboys fulfilled and which had been passed on to me, in turn,
to celebrate in honorable solidarity with the great people in togas. I obviously
didn't feel all this with such clear awareness, but from then on I never entered
Tia Marta's without holding my head high and thinking with heroic vainglory,
'The Romans did this too!' I wasn't much taller than a Gothic sword at the time
and I was in love with a fat woman who lived at the end of the street . . ."

Farther on in that same letter Fradique adds, "My love of Unity was, therefore, what in fact led me to History: a love that involves a horror of interruptions, gaps, dark spaces where one is ignorant of what's there. I traveled all through the parts of the world where it is possible to travel; I read all the books on explorations and journeys, because it was distasteful to me not to know the globe I inhabited right down to its very limits and not to feel the continuous solidarity of the piece of land I had under my feet with every other land curving out there beyond. That's why I explore history so tirelessly, in order to perceive to its very last limits the humanity to which I belong and to feel a tight solidarity of my being with that of all those who went before me in life. Maybe you're muttering disdainfully, 'Mere nosiness!' Don't disdain being nosy, my friend. It's a human impulse that has infinite breadth and which, like all of them, goes from the contemptible to the sublime. On the one hand it leads people to listen at doorways and on the other to discover America!"

Fradique's historical knowledge was really surprising for its depth and detail. A friend of ours exclaimed one day, with that affable irony that in men of the Celtic race stresses and corrects admiration, "That Fradique! He'll pick up his cigar box along with a profound and crystal-clear synthesis of the Peloponnesian War and then light his cigar and explain the craftsmanship of the metal work on Leonidas's belt buckle!" Indeed, his strong capacity for understanding collective movements philosophically and his keen ability to evoke individual characteristics psychologically was joined in him to a minute archeological knowledge of the life, customs, dress, weapons, festivals, and rites of all ages, from Vedic India to Imperial France. His letters to Oliveira Martins (on Sebastianism, our Empire in the East, the Marquis of Pombal) are truly marvelous for their wise intuition, their high synthetic power, the certainty of their knowledge, and the strength and abundance of their new ideas.* And, in addition, his archeological erudition repeatedly clarified and helped old Suma Rabema in the patient and delicate reconstruction of the customs and manners of classical antiquity in the composition of his canvases. Suma Rabema confessed this to me one afternoon while watering the rosebushes in his Chelsea garden.

Fradique was aided, furthermore, by a prodigious memory, one that took in everything and retained everything, a vast, well-lighted storeroom of facts, notions, and forms, all carefully gathered and classified, always at the ready. Our

---

*[Note in the original] These letters constitute true historical essays, which, because of their length, could not be included in this collection. Together with some scattered notes and fragments, they will make up a volume whose compiler is going to call it, I think, "The Poetry and Prose of Fradique Mendes."

friend Chambray stated that for anything comparable to Fradique's memory in matters of "installation, order, and excellence of stock," he could only think of the wine cellar at the Café Inglês.

Fradique's culture kept receiving constant nourishment and growth from the endless string of trips he took under the impulse of intellectual curiosity and admiration. Archeology alone would take him to the East four times, although his last stay of eighteen months in Jerusalem was motivated (according to what Consul Raccolini told me) by a poetic love affair with one of the most splendid women of Syria, a daughter of Abraham Coppo, the wealthy banker from Aleppo, who unfortunately later died in the shipwreck of the *Magnolia* along the sad coast of Cyprus. His adventurous and difficult pilgrimage to China, from Tibet (where he almost left his life behind in a foolhardy attempt to penetrate the holy city of Lhasa) to upper Manchuria, brought out the most complete study ever undertaken up till now by a European of the customs, government, ethics, and literature of that people, "the most profound among all (according to Fradique), who have managed to discover the only three or four moral principles that can eternalize a civilization by their absolute strength."

The examination of Russia and its social and religious movements took him on prolonged trips through the rural provinces that lay between the Dnieper and the Volga. The need for certainty regarding the penal colonies in Siberia impelled him to confront hundreds of miles of steppes and snow in a crude telega, all the way to the silver mines of Nerchinski. And he would have continued with this active interest had he not suddenly received, on reaching the coast at Archangel, this dispatch from General Armankoff, the head of Section IV of the Imperial Police: *Monsieur, vous nous observez de trop près pour que votre jugement n'en soit faussé; je vous invite donc, sur votre intérêt, et pour avoir de la Russie une vue d'ensemble plus exacte, d'aller le regarder de plus loin, dans votre belle maison de Paris!*[12] Fradique departed hastily for Vaasa, on the Gulf of Bothnia. He immediately passed over to Sweden and from there sent this undated note to General Armankoff: *Monsieur, j'ai reçu votre invitation où il y a beaucoup d'intolérance et trois fautes de français.*[13]

The same interests of mind and "needs for certainty" took him to cross South America from the Amazon to the sands of Patagonia and South Africa from the Cape to the mountains of Zokunga . . . "I have leafed through and attentively read the world as if it were a book full of ideas. To see things *outwardly*, as a mere feast for the eyes, I went only to Morocco."

What rendered these fruitful trips into a learning experience was his quick and loving sympathy for all the peoples he encountered. He never visited countries the way the detestable French tourist does, noting from up on high and in a withering way their "defects"—that is, their divergences from the kind of mediocre and generic civilization from which he came and which he prefers. Fradique would immediately fall in love with the customs, ideas, and prejudices of the people around him and, blending in with their ways of thinking and feeling, he would receive a direct and living lesson from every society into which he had plunged. The efficient doctrine of "when in Rome do as the Romans do," so easy and sweet to effect when in Rome among the vineyards of the Celian Hill and the Pauline Fountain, he would fulfill with pleasure while plodding along in his torn sandals through the passes of the Himalayas. And he was just as much at home in a philosophical beer garden in Germany, delving deeply into the Absolute among professors from Tübingen, as in an African outpost in the land of the Matabele, comparing the merits of the Express carbine with that of the Winchester among elephant hunters.

From 1880 on, his movements were slowly becoming centered between Paris and London, with the exception of "filial visits" to Portugal, because, in spite of his wanderings about the world, the ease with which he became nationalized in alien lands, and his critical impersonality, Fradique always remained a genuine Portuguese, with the inerasable traits of an insular nobleman.

The purest and most intimate part of his interest he always gave to men and matters Portuguese. He had undertaken the purchase of the Saragoça estate in Sintra (as he says in a letter to F. G., with unaccustomed emotion) "to *own some land in Portugal* and to tie myself with a strong link to the august soil whence my forebears had set out, drawn by an ingenuous tumult of grand ideas, as seekers of worlds from whom I have inherited my blood and a curiosity for the *beyond*!"

Whenever he came to Portugal, he would "fortify his fiber" by riding slowly through a province on horseback, lingering in decrepit hamlets that enchanted him, conversing endlessly by rustic hearths, fraternizing noisily in churchyards and taverns, taking festive trips on pilgrimages by oxcart, an ancient and venerable Sabine cart draped with chintz and decorated with laurel. The region he liked best was the Ribatejo, that level land of marshes and cattle. "There (he says), wearing a short jacket with a sash, mounted on a colt, holding up a herdsman's prod and riding among the herds of cattle in the fresh and delicate morning air, I feel the delights of living more than anywhere else in the world."

He liked Lisbon only as a landscape. "With three strong finishing touches (he wrote me from the Hotel Braganza in 1881)—a grove of trees and gentle pines planted on the bald hills of the Other Bank, gleaming and merry tiles cloaking the dirty row-house fronts, and a thorough sweeping of these blessed streets—Lisbon could be one of those beauties of Nature that man has created and which become a motive for dreams, art, and pilgrimages. Yet, I don't feel that I could tolerate an existence rooted in Lisbon. What's lacking here is an intellectual atmosphere where the soul can breathe. Also, certain singularly repugnant traits dominate. Lisbon is a city that is *pseudoliterary, boorish, foppish,* and *lawyerish.* The simple way in which a clerk sells a yard of ribbon is literary and in the 'thank you' with which a lady receives it there is a *boorishness* that shows through. There's something lawyerish even in art and there's *foppishness* even in cemeteries. But the supreme nausea, my friend, is brought on by politicking and politickers."

Fradique nourished a thoroughgoing horror of politicians, much of it unjustified: an intellectual horror, judging them to be ignorant, coarse, and absolutely inept for the creation or understanding of ideas; a worldly horror, presuming them to be shabby, crass in manners, and out of place among people of taste; a physical horror, imagining that they never washed or changed their socks and that they gave off that soft, limp odor that so startles and nauseates upon entering the Parliament those who are not used to it out of professional habit.

There were certainly specks of perfect truth in these fierce opinions, but in general Fradique's judgments on politics offered the stamp of a prejudice that becomes dogmatic and doesn't come from any discriminating observation. That was how I put it to him one morning at the Braganza, showing him that all those deficiencies of spirit, culture, manners, taste, and gentility which he so harshly noted in politicians can be sufficiently explained by the hasty democratization of our society, by the abject vulgarity of provincial life, by the abominable influences of the university, and even by essentially honest but hidden reasons for those unfortunate politicians chosen by avenging fate for the destruction of our land.

Fradique replied simply, "If a dead mouse were to tell me 'I stink for this or that reason but mostly because I'm rotting,' I still wouldn't stop having him swept out of my bedroom."

There was an instinctive antipathy here, completely physiological, whose intransigence and obstinacy could be overcome neither by facts nor by reason. Much more justified was the horror inspired in him by the social life of Lisbon, its clumsy, extreme, and silly imitation of Paris. That "yokel aping," masterfully denounced by him in a letter he wrote me in 1885, where he stipulates in a luminous summation that *"Lisbon is a city translated from the French into slang,"* became a real torture for him as soon as his train reached the Santa Apolónia station. He was always anxious then to discover some trace of the genuine Portugal through that trumpery of Frenchiness.

Food immediately became a real displeasure for him and at every moment in his letters and conversation he would bemoan his being unable to find a "vernacular meal." "Where (he exclaims somewhere) are the venerable dishes of Portuguese Portugal: duck with macaroni from the eighteenth century, the indigestible and divine meatballs from the time of the Discoveries, or those wonderful chicken giblets, the favorite tidbit of King John IV in the astonished report delivered to London by the English noblemen who had come to the kingdom to fetch the bride of Charles II? All of it had been corrupted! The same shabby provincialism translates into slang the comedies of Labiche and the delicacies of Gouffé. And here we are, feeding miserably on the democratic leftovers from the boulevards, warmed over and served with mockery and aspic! A strange disaster! The most delicious fare in Portugal—pork loin, Lafões veal, vegetables, desserts, wines—have degenerated ever since the coming of constitutionalism and parliamentarianism. With those sinister grafts onto the old Lusitanian trunk, fruits have lost their taste, just as men have lost their character . . ."

On only one occasion did I see him completely satisfied in this well-considered matter. It was in a tavern (where I had taken him) in the Mouraria, as he looked down at a complicated and profound dish of codfish, peppers, and chickpeas. In order to enjoy it properly, Fradique took off his jacket. And since one of us threw out the name of Renan as we attacked that unequalled tidbit, Fradique protested passionately:

"No ideas! Let me savor this meal of codfish with perfect innocence of spirit, as in the time of John V, before there was any democracy or criticism!"

Nostalgia for the old Portugal was constant in him and he believed the world diminished for having lost this kind of intensely original civilization. This love for the past would revive in him in a rather curious way when he saw emerge in Lisbon, with an original inspiration, the luxury and the intelligent "modernism" of civilizations more imbued with culture and perfect taste. The last time I ran into him in Lisbon was in the Rato, at a soirée of rare and delicate brilliance. Fradique looked desolate.

"In Paris," he said, "the Duchess of La Rochefoucauld-Bisaccia can give a soirée just like this and therefore it's not worth the trouble for me to spend Lent in Marvão. Just suppose, however, that I happen here to come upon a soirée from the time of Queen Maria I, at the house of the Marialvas, with noble ladies seated on mats, monks playing the lundum on the mandolin, high magistrates requesting themes for poetic improvisation, and lackeys in the courtyard among beggars chanting the litany in a chorus! . . . That would be something unique and delightful for which I would make the trip from Paris in a litter!"

One day, when we were dining at the home of Carlos Mayer and Fradique was lamenting with sincere melancholy about the old Portugal with its noblemen and friars in the time of John V, Ramalho Ortigão was unable to contain himself.

"You're a monster, Fradique! What you'd like would to be living in comfortable mid-nineteenth-century Paris and have here, two days' journey away, the Portugal of the eighteenth century where you come as to a museum and rejoice in the picturesque and the archaic . . . You, there on the rue de Varennes, comforted by decency and order, and we here in stinky alleys, flooded at night with the dumping of foul sewage, intimidated by the street riots of the Marquis de Cascais or the Count de Aveiras, shoved into a dungeon by thuggish police, and so on and so forth . . . Confess that that's what you want!"

Fradique calmly replied, "It would have been more worthy and patriotic that instead of seeing you here, you men of letters, all dressed up in the neckties and ideas that all Europe wears, to have found you in wigs and pigtails, with the ancient pockets of your silk jackets stuffed with Sapphic odes, huddling in wholesome fear of King and Devil and frequenting the courtyards of Marialva and Aveiro with hopes that those of higher station, after receiving thanks, would send you by a little black servant boy the leftovers of their turkeys along with a topic to write about. All of that would be worthily Portuguese and sincere. You couldn't deserve anything better and life isn't possible without a bit of the picturesque as dessert."

In fact, in that longing of Fradique's for ancient Portugal there was a love for the picturesque, something strange in a man so subjective and intellectual, but above all there was a hatred of this universal modernization that reduces all customs, beliefs, ideas, tastes, styles, the most innate and most original characteristics, to a kind of uniform (represented by the *utilitarian and serious* fellow in a black frock coat), much like the monotony that the Chinese bring on as they trim the trees in a garden until they reach the unique and dogmatic shape of a pyramid or a funerary urn.

For that reason, in Portugal Fradique had special love for the people, who didn't change, the same way as the nature that surrounds them and passes on to them its grave and gentle characteristics, which likewise don't change. He loved them for their qualities and also for their defects: for their drowsy patience of a gentle ox, for the idyllic joy with which they make a poem out of work, for their calm submission to the vassalage, which after *Milord King* venerates *Milord*

Government, for their amiable and natural sweetness, for their pagan Catholicism and faithful love for the Latin gods who have been turned into calendar saints, for their dress, for their songs . . . "I love them, too (he says), for their speech, so rough and so poor, but the only one in Portugal where one doesn't feel the hateful influence of Lamartinism or of dog-eared lecture notes on Public Law."

VI

The last time Fradique visited Lisbon was when I met him in the Rato, as he mourned over the pious and dandified soirées of the eighteenth century. The onetime poet of the *Inscriptions* was fifty years old at the time and had been taken more and more by the quiet smoothness of his Parisian habits.

Fradique had been living on the rue de Varennes since 1880, in a wing of the former palace of the Dukes of Tredennes, which he had furnished with sober, grave luxury, having always detested that heaping together of embellishments and stuffing, where art and centuries are all confused and contradicting each other, and which, under the barbarous and just name of bric-a-brac, so seduces financiers and cocottes. Noble and rich tapestries of landscapes and history, broad divans from Aubusson, some pieces of furniture in the style of the French Renaissance, rare porcelains from Delft and China, space, light, and a harmony of tones—there you have what was to be found in the five rooms that made up Fradique's "lair." All the balconies, of iron lacework and dating from Louis XIV, opened onto one of those gardens with ancient trees which, in that noble and ecclesiastical district, form retreats of silent and sylvan peace and where sometimes on May nights a nightingale ventures a song.

Fradique's life was measured by an age-old clock, which preceded the slow and almost austere tolling of the hour with the silver notes of an ancient court dance and was maintained in an unchanging regularity by his servant Smith, an old Scot from the clan of the Macduffs, whose hair was now completely white but whose flesh was still pink and who for thirty years had accompanied him with a strict zeal through life and the world.

At nine o'clock in the morning, as soon as the gentle and melancholy rhythms of that forgotten minuet by Cimarosa or Haydn spread out, Smith would burst into Fradique's bedroom, open all the windows to the light, and shout, "Morning, Sir!" Fradique would immediately make a quick leap from under the covers, a thing he considered "of transcendent importance for one's hygiene," and run to the huge marble washbasin, rinsing his face and head in cold water with all the snorting of a happy Triton. Then, putting on one of the silk tunics that impressed me so much and stretching out in an easy chair, he turned himself over to Smith, who as a barber (as Fradique stated) combined the deft touch of Figaro and the confidential wisdom of Louis XI's Oliveiro. And, as a matter of fact, while he was lathering and shaving him, Smith went along reciting a detailed, neat, and solid summary, replete with facts, from the political dispatches in the *Times*, the *Standard*, and the *Cologne Gazette*.

For me it was always a refreshing and delightful surprise to see Smith, with his high, white Palmerstone collar, short jacket, green and black plaid trousers (the colors of his clan), and low-cut patent leather shoes, passing the brush over his master's chin and saying softly, with perfect skill and with perfect knowledge, "The meeting between Prince Bismarck and Count Kalnocky isn't going to take place . . . The Conservatives lost the special election in York . . . There was talk in Vienna yesterday of a new Russian loan . . ." Friends in Lisbon would laugh at this "parroting," but Fradique maintained that there was a beneficial return here to the classical tradition that held all across the Latin world after Scipio Africanus instituted the practice of having barbers as the "universal informants of public affairs." These short summaries of Smith's formed the framework of Fradique's political notions, and he never said, "I read in the *Times*," but "I read in Smith."

Well-shaven and well-informed, Fradique would plunge into a lukewarm bath, where he returned to the care of the vigorous hands of Smith, who, equipped with a set of gloves of wool, flannel, tow, horsehair, and tiger skin, would massage him until his whole body was like Apollo's, "pink and glowing." Then he would have his chocolate and settle down in his library, a serious and simple room, where an image of Truth, radiantly white in her marble nudity, was placing her finger over her pure lips, symbolizing across a wide ebony table the thoroughly intimate work of the search for truths that are not meant for noise or for the world.

At one o'clock he would eat for lunch some eggs and vegetables, with all the sobriety of a Greek, and then, lying on a divan and taking slow sips of Russian tea, he would go through the newspapers and magazines, reading the columns on art, literature, theater, and society, which were not within Smith's political purview. He would also read with care the Portuguese papers (which somewhere he calls "picaresque phenomena of social decomposition"), always in character but of especial interest to someone like him, who took pleasure in analyzing "the genuine and sincere work of mediocrity" and considered Callinus just as worthy of study as Voltaire. The rest of the day he gave over to friends, visitors, studios, fencing societies, exhibitions, clubs—in a word, to the diverse cares that a man of high taste creates for himself in a city of high civilization.

In the afternoon he would go up to the Bois, driving his phaeton or mounted on Sabá, a wonderful mare from the stud farm of Ain Weibah, which the Emir of Mossul had given him. And his evening (when he wasn't filling a seat at the opera or at the Comédie) was spent in some salon, always needing to end his day in the midst of the "ephemeral feminine" (as Fradique would say).

The influence of this "feminine" was supreme for his existence. Fradique loved women, but beyond them and above all things, he loved Woman.

His approach to women was governed jointly by the devotions of a spiritualist, the curiosity of a critic, and the demands of a full-blooded person. Like the sentimentalists of the Restoration, Fradique considered them superior "organisms," divinely complicated, different and more worthy of adoration than everything else Nature has to offer. At the same time, in this cult he would go about dissecting and studying that "divine organism" fiber by fiber, without respect, with the passion of an analyst; and frequently both the enthusiast and the critic would disappear, leaving in him only a man loving a woman in the simple and good natural law, as the fauns loved the nymphs.

Women for him, in addition to this, were (at least in his conversational theories) classified into species. There was the "exterior woman," a flower of luxury and cultured worldliness; and there was the "interior woman," the one who watches over the home, before whom, no matter how attractive, Fradique maintained a tone filled with respect, excluding all experimental investigation. "In their presence (he writes Madame de Jouarre) I am as though I were handling someone else's wax-sealed letter." In the presence of those who "exteriorize" themselves and live completely in the midst of noise and panache, however, Fradique was as free and irresponsible as when facing a printed book. "Thumbing through the pages (he says, still to Madame Jouarre), making notes on its silky margins, criticizing it aloud with independence and verve, taking it home in a coupé to read at night, recommending it to a friend, tossing it into a corner after the best pages have been read—all that is quite permissible, I believe, according to the primer and the book of rules."

Could these subtleties (as a cruel friend of ours suggested) be those of a man who theorizes and idealizes his temperament of a porter in order to make it into something of literary interest? I don't know. The most instructive commentary on his theories he would give off when appearing in a salon, in the midst of the "ephemeral feminine." Certain very voluptuous women, when listening to a man who makes them uneasy, without realizing it will open their lips. With Fradique it was the eyes that grew wider. His were small and tobacco-brown, but when next to one of these exterior women, "stars of worldliness," they became huge, filled with a dark velvety glow, almost damp. The old Lady Mongrave compared them to "the open gullets of two snakes." What was there, in fact, was an act of enticement and absorption, but above all there was evidence of the perturbation and enchantment that filled him. In that attention, which a pious person shows before the Virgin, in the warm whispers of a voice more mollifying than a gust of hot air from a hearth, in the perplexed moistening of his delicate eyes, women only saw the omnipotent and conquering influence of their charms of form and spirit on a splendidly virile man. And there is no man more dangerous than the one who always gives women a clear and almost tangible impression that they are irresistible, that they can conquer the most recalcitrant heart with nothing but a slow movement of the shoulders or whispering "What a lovely afternoon!" The one who shows himself easily seduced easily becomes the seducer. It is the Indian legend, so wise and so true, of the magic mirror in which old Maharani saw herself radiantly beautiful. In order to get and keep that mirror where her wrinkled skin is reflected with so much splendor, what sins and betrayals will Maharani not commit? . . .

I believe, then, that Fradique was deeply loved and that he deserved it magnificently. Women found something in that creature that was rare among men— a Man. And for them Fradique possessed that inestimable superiority, almost unheard of in our generation, of an extremely sensitive soul served by an extremely strong body.

More enduring and intense than his loves, however, were the friendships that Fradique drew to himself by his moral excellence. When I met him for the first time in Lisbon, in the remote year of 1867, I thought I had sensed in his nature (the same as in his poetry) a brilliant and steely impassivity, and with the admiration that his art, personality, vigor, and silk tunic had left in me, I confessed to J. Teixeira de Azevedo one day that I hadn't found in the poet of the *Inscriptions* that *warm milk of human kindness* for which old Shakespeare (and I after him) understood a man to be worthy of humanity. His very polish, so smiling and perfect, seemed to me to be made of a system rather than being genuinely inborn. My formation of this judgment was backed up by a letter (old, already, from 1855) someone had entrusted to me and in which Fradique, with all the light haughtiness of youth, threw out this rude program of behavior: "Men were born to work, women to weep, and we, the strong, to pass coldly along our way . . ."

But in 1880, when our intimacy had become established, one night at a table in the Bignon (Fradique was fifty), either because I was observing him with more penetration at that time or because already working in him with age was that phenomenon that Fustan de Carmanges later called *le dégel de Fradique*,[14] quite soon I could feel emerging through the marble impassivity of the carver of the *Inscriptions*, warmly and generously, *the milk of human kindness*.

The strong expression of virtue in him that impressed me at once was an unconditional and unrestricted indulgence. Either as a conclusion of his philosophy or as an inspiration of his nature, Fradique, in the face of sin or crime, would lean toward that old Evangelical mercy which, aware of universal fragility, asks from where the hand pure enough to cast the first stone against the sin will arise. He saw in all guilt (perhaps against his better reason, but obeying that *voice* that whispered to Saint Francis and still speaks) an irremediable human weakness and his forgiveness would emerge immediately from the depths of the mercy that lay in his soul like a spring of pure water in rich soil, always about to burst forth.

His goodness, however, wasn't limited to this passive expression. All misfortune, from the limited and tangible bitterness that occurs on the streets to the vast and widespread misery that with elemental force devastates classes and races, found a diligent and true consoler in him. These are the noble words he wrote in his last years (in a letter to G. F.): "All of us who live on this globe make up an immense caravan that is marching confusedly toward Nothingness, surrounded by an impassive Nature, mortal like us, which doesn't understand or even see us and from which we cannot hope for either succor or consolation. All that remains for us to do is follow the path along which that centuries-old precept, the divine summation of all human experience, carries us: 'Help ye one another!' So that on this tumultuous journey, where countless steps are mingled, each one will give half his loaf to the one who is hungry, hand half his cloak to the one who is cold, lend his arm to the one who is about to stumble, raise up the body of the one who has already fallen, and if someone is better provided for and sure of his path but stands only in need of the sympathy of other souls, let those souls open up to him and pour out that sympathy . . . Only then will we succeed in lending some beauty and some dignity to this dark flight toward Death."

Fradique was certainly not a militant saint who sought out misery in alleyways that was in need of rescue, but there was never any evil as he saw it that wouldn't receive relief from his part. Whenever he happened to read in the paper about some calamity or indigence he would use a pencil to mark a number on the margin, indicating to old Smith the number of pounds to be sent, quietly and without any publicity. His maxim concerning the poor (whom economists assert do not deserve charity but justice) was that "One coin in the hand at mealtime is worth two high-flying philosophies." Children especially, when in need, would bring out an infinite tenderness in him: he was that very rare kind of person who, when encountering on a harsh winter's day a begging child run through with cold, stops in the wind and rain to patiently unbutton his coat and patiently take off his gloves and digs into his pockets for a silver coin that will be the child's warmth and daily bread.

This charity reached out in a Buddhistic way to everything alive. I knew of no man more respectful of animals and their rights. On one occasion in Paris, when we were both running to a stand of fiacres to get out of the downpour that had opened up and hurry on to a tapestry auction (where Fradique had his eyes on *Nine Muses Dancing among the Laurels*), all we could find was a coupé whose old nag, his feedbag over his nose, was melancholy eating his ration. Fradique insisted on waiting until the horse had peacefully eaten his lunch, and he lost the *Nine Muses*.

He has been especially concerned of late with the poverty of the lower classes, feeling that in these industrial and materialistic democracies of ours, furiously involved in the selfish struggle for bread, every day souls are becoming more barren and less capable of pity. "Brotherhood (he says in a letter from 1886 that I have kept) is sinking low, especially in these vast hives of brick and mortar where men insist on piling up and fighting among themselves; and, with a constant decline in rustic customs and simplicity, the world is rolling along to a state of ferocious selfishness. The first evidence of this selfishness is in the noisy development of philanthropy. When charity becomes organized, consolidated as an institution with rules, reports, committees, meetings, a presiding officer and a little bell, and goes from being a natural feeling to an official function, it is because man can no longer rely on the impulses of his heart and must publicly oblige himself to doing good according to the prescriptions of a statute. With hearts hardened like that and with winters so long, what will become of the poor?"

How many times in my presence on late November afternoons in his library, lighted only by the uncertain and gentle flame of the wood in the fireplace, would Fradique emerge from a silence in which his gaze had been off in the distance, as though sinking into a sad horizon, and would lament, with tender elevation, all human misery! He would reiterate then his bitter realization of the growing harshness of mankind, driven by the violence of conflict and competition to a state of crude selfishness, where everyone becomes a wolf to his fellow, *homo homini lupus*.

"What is needed is for another Christ to come," I whispered one day.

Fradique shrugged his shoulders, saying:

"He will come. Perhaps he will free the slaves. For this he will have his church and his liturgy, and then he will be denied and later he will be forgotten, and finally new crowds of slaves will arise. There is nothing to be done. What is left is for everyone, from prudence, to put some money together and buy a revolver and to his fellows who knock on his door give, according to the circumstances, either bread or a bullet."

In that way, full of ideas, performing gentle tasks and pleasant works, Fradique Mendes's final years in Paris went along until, in the winter of 1888, death took him in the form that he, like Caesar, had always looked forward to, *inopinatam atque repentinam.*[15]

One night, on leaving a soirée given by the Countess de la Ferté (an old friend of Fradique's, with whom he had taken a yacht trip to Iceland), he found in the cloakroom that his Russian fur coat had been mistaken for another, also comfortable and rich, which had in its pocket a wallet with the monogram and cards of General Terran-d'Azy. Fradique, who suffered from intolerable dislikes, refused to wrap himself up in the warm covering of that cantankerous and grippe-ridden officer, and he crossed the Place de la Concorde on foot, wearing only his dinner jacket, until he reached the Rue Royale Club. The night was dry and clear but cut through by one of those soft winds, more delicate than a breath, which had honed itself over the leagues it had crossed from the snow-covered plains of the north and which old André Vasali had compared to a "treacherous dagger." The next day he awoke with a slight cough. Indifferent to any protection, however, and sure of the robustness with which he had confronted so much inclement weather, he went to Fontainebleau with some friends, up on a mail coach. Later that night, on retiring, he had a long and intense attack of chills and shivering and thirty hours later, without any suffering, so peaceful that for a long time Smith had thought he was asleep, Fradique, as the ancients used to say, "had lived." A beautiful summer day could not have ended more sweetly.

Dr. Labert declared that it had been a very rare form of pleurisy. And he added with a precise sense of human good fortune, *Toujours de la chance, ce Fradique!*[16]

He was accompanied on his last journey through the streets of Paris, under a gray, snowy sky, by some of the grandest men of France in matters of knowledge and art. Pretty faces, trod on now by time, wept for him with nostalgia for emotions long gone by. And in poor homes, around hearths where there was no fire, this skeptic with an elegant hand who took care of human ills while wrapped in a silk dressing gown was most certainly mourned too.

He lies in Père-Lachaise, not far from the grave of Balzac, where on All Souls' Day he would always place a bouquet of those violets from Parma that the creator of *The Human Comedy* loved so much. Faithful hands, in their turn, always keep the simple stone that covers him in the ground perfumed with fresh roses.

VII

The learned moralist who signs himself Alceste, in the *Gazette de Paris*, dedicated a column to Fradique Mendes in which he sums up his spirit and his actions in this way: "A truly personal and strong thinker, Fradique Mendes did not leave any written work. From indifference and from indolence, this man squandered his enormous intellectual wealth. From the block of gold out of which he might have carved an imperishable monument he cut slices and crumbs over the years, which he scattered about liberally, conversing in the salons and clubs of Paris. All this gold dust has been lost in ordinary dust. Above Fradique's tomb, as over that of the unknown Greek about whom the *Anthology* sings, there could be written, 'Here lies the sound of the wind that passed, scattering perfume, warmth, and seeds to no avail'. . ."

The entire article was done with the usual superficiality and lack of consideration of the French, reflected in the designations *indolence* and *indifference*, no less, which kept coming up in that ornate and pompous page, as though giving a precise mark to Fradique's nature. He was, on the contrary, a man of passion, action, and unremitting labor. And a man like him, who had taken part in two campaigns, was the apostle of a religion, and who had traveled across the five continents, had absorbed so many civilizations, had covered all the knowledge of his time, could scarcely be accused of *indolence* and *indifference*.

The chronicler of the *Gazette de Paris*, however, is right on target when he states that the tireless worker left no works. The only thing, in fact, that we know of his in print and in circulation is the poetry of the *Inscriptions*, published in the *Revolução de Setembro*, and that strange little poem in barbarous Latin, "Laus Veneris Tenebrosae," which appeared in the *Revue de Poésie et d'Art*, founded toward the end of 1869 by a group of Symbolist poets. Fradique did leave manuscripts, however. Many times, on the rue de Varennes, I caught sight of them in a Spanish case with ironwork braces from the fourteenth century that Fradique called his Potter's Field. All those papers (and their entire disposition) were bequeathed by Fradique to that *Libuska* of whom he speaks at great length in his letters to Madame de Jouarre and who becomes so familiar and real for us with "her velvety white tresses of a Venetian lady and her large Juno-esque eyes."

That lady, whose name was Varia Lobrinska, was of the old Russian family of the Princes of Palidoff. In 1874 her husband, Paul Lobrinski, a silent and vague diplomat who had belonged to the Imperial Guards regiment and would write "capiténe" for *capitaine*, had died in Paris toward the end of autumn, while still young, from a languid and long anemia. Madame Lobrinska, with solemn grief and surrounded by maidservants and mourning crepe, immediately retired to her vast Russian estates near Starobelsk in the governorate of Kharkov. With spring, however, she returned, along with the flowers on the chestnut trees, and ever since lived in Paris in a luxurious and merry widowhood. One day at Madame de Jouarre's she met Fradique, who at the time was enraptured by a cult of Slavic literatures and was passionately busying himself with the oldest and noblest of their poems, *The Judgment of Libuska*, discovered by chance in 1818 in the archives of the Zelene Hora castle. Madame Lobrinska was a relative of the masters of Zelene Hora, the Counts of Colloredo, and she just happened to own a copy of the two leaves of parchment that contain the old barbaric epic.

They read that heroic text together until that sweet moment came in which, as with Dante's two lovers, "they read no more the entire day." Fradique had given Madame Lobrinska the name Libuska, the queen who appears in the *Judgment* "dressed in white and resplendent with wisdom." She called Fradique Lucifer. The poet of the *Inscriptions* died that November and days later Madame Lobrinska retired once again to her melancholy estate near Starobelsky, in the governorate of Kharkov. Her friends smiled and whispered sympathetically that Madame Lobrinska had fled and gone to weep her second widowhood among her muzhiks until the lilacs bloomed again. But this time Libuska didn't return, not even with the flowering of the chestnut trees.

Madame Lobrinska's husband had been a diplomat who mainly studied and practiced menus and cotillions. His career was, therefore, irreparably subaltern and slow. For six years he lounged about Rio de Janeiro and the groves of Petrópolis as secretary, awaiting that legation in Europe which Prince Gortchakoff, then Imperial foreign minister, had said belonged to Madame Lobrinska par *droit de beauté et de sagesse*.[17] The legation in Europe, in a worldly, cultured capital without banana trees, never came as compensation for those exiles who suffered from a nostalgia for snow, but Madame Lobrinska in her exile came to learn our soft language of Portugal so thoroughly that Fradique showed me a translation of Lavoski's elegy "The Hill of Goodbye" she had put together with superior purity and relief. Only she, among all of Fradique's women friends, could appreciate as living pages, in which the thinker had set down the secrets of his thoughts, those manuscripts that for the others would have been nothing but dry, dead sheets of paper covered with incomprehensible lines of writing.

As soon as I started gathering up Fradique Mendes's scattered letters I wrote to Madame Lobrinska, telling her of my strong desire to establish by means of a loving study the features of that transcendental spirit, and I begged her for, if not a few extracts from his manuscripts, at least some revelations about *his nature*. Madame Lobrinska's reply was a well-determined and well-deduced refusal, showing that behind those "clear eyes of a Juno" there was the clear mind of a Minerva. "The papers of Carlos Fradique (she said in summation) had been entrusted to her, who lived far removed from publicity and a world interested in the profits of that publicity, with the intention that they would preserve forever more the intimate and secret character in which Fradique had kept them for so long, and under those conditions *to reveal his nature* would be manifestly contrary to the intimate and proud feeling that had dictated that bequest . . ." This came written in a thick, round hand on a large sheet of rough paper where in one corner, gleaming in gold under a golden crown, there was this device: *Per terram ad coelum.*[18]

In this way the obscurity that surrounds Fradique's manuscripts was established. What was really contained in that iron chest that Fradique, with disconsolate pride, had called his Potter's Field, judging the thoughts that he tossed in there to be so poor and to have no glitter for the world?

Some friends think that among his things they would have found sketched out at least, or even completed, the two works that Fradique had alluded to as the ones most captivating for an artist or a thinker in this century, a *Psychology of Religions* and a *Theory of the Will.*

Others (like J. Teixeira de Azevedo) felt that in those papers there was a novel of epic realism, the reconstruction of an extinct civilization, like *Salammbô*. They deduced that (unpleasant) supposition from a letter to Oliveira Martins from 1880, where Fradique exclaimed with mysterious irony: "I feel myself slipping, my dear historian, into vain and blameworthy practices. Woe is me, woe is me, as my pen is running away from me into evil. What malignant demon, covered with the dust of the ages and carrying archeological in-folios under his arm, came whispering to me, on one of these nights of winter cold and decorative erudition, 'Put a novel together. And in your novel bring Oriental antiquity back to life'!? And his suggestions seemed sweet to me, my friend, with a lethal sweetness. What would you say, my fine Oliveira Martins, if one day, without warning, you were to receive a volume of mine, printed with solemnity and beginning with these lines: '*Once upon a time in Babylonia, during the month of Sivanu, after the harvest of the balms . . .*'? You, of course (I can sense it from here) would cover your face with trembling hands and mutter, 'Good Lord! Here comes the description of the temple of the Seven Spheres, with all its terraces, the description of the Battle of Halub, with all its weapons, the description of Sennacherib's banquet, with all its delicacies! . . . Neither the embroidery of a single tunic nor the reliefs on a single cup will be spared us! And he calls himself a close friend!'"

Ramalho Ortigão, on the contrary, tends to believe that the papers of Fradique contain *Memoirs*, because only on *Memoirs* one can coherently impose the condition of remaining secret.

I, for my part and from a better and more continuous acquaintance with Fradique, have concluded that he left neither a book on psychology nor an archeological epic (which would certainly have seemed to Fradique a blameworthy and ostentatious display of picturesque and easy knowledge), nor any *Memoirs*, inexplicable in a man who was all ideas and abstraction and who hid his life with such high-minded modesty. And I firmly attest that in that iron chest lost off in an old Russian estate there is no work, because Fradique was never truly an *author*.

Not that he lacked the ideas needed to be one, but he did lack the certainty that they had a *definitive* value to be worth written down and perpetuated, and he also lacked the patient art or the strong desire for that form he had conceived in the abstract as being the only one worthy, because of some rare and special beauty, of giving embodiment to his ideas. There was a mistrust of himself as a thinker whose conclusions, as they renovated philosophy and science, might imprint an unexpected movement on the human spirit; and a mistrust of himself as a writer and creator of a prose that for itself alone and separate from the value of the thought would exercise upon souls the ineffable action of the absolutely beautiful. There you have the two negative influences that held Fradique back, keeping him always unpublished and mute. He wanted everything that emanated from his intelligence to act perpetually upon the intelligence of others for its definitive truth or its incomparable beauty. But the inclement and sage criticism that he practiced on others he also practiced on himself every day, with redoubled sagacity and inclemency. The feeling for reality, so alive in him, caused him to distinguish his own spirit for just what it was, with its real power and its real limits, without its appearing to him more powerful or broader due to those "wisps of literary illusion" that bring every man of letters, as soon as pen runs across paper, to take for gleaming rays of light some few meager scratches of ink. And concluding that neither with ideas nor with form could he bring to other intelligences any persuasion or charm that would make its definitive mark in the evolution of reason or taste, he preferred proudly to remain silent. For reasons nobly different from those of Descartes, in that way he followed the maxim that had so seduced the latter, *bene vixit qui bene latuit.*[19]

None of these feelings did he confess to me, but I caught them all quite clearly on one of the last Christmases I got to spend on the rue de Varennes, where Fradique had put me up for New Year's with undeserved splendor. It was a great, stormy winter night, and after coffee, our legs stretched out in front of the tall flames from the beechwood logs in the hearth, we were chatting about Africa and African religions. In the Zambezi region Fradique had gathered some very sharp and lively notes on native cults, which concerned the deification of dead chiefs, transformed by death into *mulungus,* spirits who dispense good and evil, with divine residence in the huts and hills where they once had had their residence in the flesh, and he compared the ceremonies and aims of these savage cults in Africa with the primitive liturgical ceremonies of the Aryans in Septa Sindhu. Fradique concluded (as he showed in a letter to Guerra Junqueiro from that time) that in religion what is real, essential, necessary, and eternal is ceremony and liturgy, and what there is of the artificial, supplementary, dispensable, and transitory is theology and morality.

All of this held me irresistibly, especially the touches of African life and nature, which he brought in as illustration, and smiling, seduced, I asked,

"Fradique, why don't you write down all this about your trip to Africa?"

It was the first time I had suggested to my friend the idea of putting a book together. He looked up with the same astonishment he would have shown had I proposed walking barefoot through the stormy night to the Bois de Marly. Then, tossing his cigarette into the fireplace, he said, sadly and slowly,

"What for? . . . I saw nothing in Africa that other people haven't seen."

And when I pointed out to him that perhaps he had seen it in a different and quite superior way, that not every day does a man educated in philosophy and imbued with erudition make a crossing through Africa, and that in science a single truth needs a thousand experimenters, Fradique was almost impatient:

"No! Neither concerning Africa nor anything else in this world do I have any conclusions that would be worth writing down so that they might change the course of history . . . All I could offer would be a series of impressions, land-scapes. And it's even worse! Because human words, as we utter them, are still impotent to embody the slightest intellectual impression or to reproduce the simple form of a bush . . . I don't know how to write! Nobody knows how to write!"

I protested laughingly against that generalization that was so rigid that it pitilessly swept everything away. And I reminded him that a few short yards away from the fireplace which was keeping us warm, in that old neighborhood of Paris where the Sorbonne, the Institut de France, and the École Normale stood, there had been many men, and there still were, who possessed, in a most perfect way, "the beautiful art of saying."

"Who?" Fradique exclaimed.

I started off with Bossuet. Fradique shrugged his shoulders in a violent show of irreverence that kept me quiet. And he immediately declared in a sharp run-down that in the two finest centuries of French literature, from *my* Bossuet to Beaumarchais, no writer had, for him, any relief, color, intensity, or life . . . And none of the moderns pleased him either. The distended thunder of Hugo was as intolerable as the oily flaccidity of Lamartine. Michelet lacked gravity and balance, Renan solidity and nerve, Taine fluidity and transparency, Flaubert vibration and heat. Poor Balzac, that one, was of a disorderly and barbaric ex-uberance. And the preciosity of the Goncourts and their world seemed perfectly indecent to him . . .

Confused, laughing, I asked that "fiercely dissatisfied" person what prose, then, did he conceive ideal and miraculous enough to deserve being written down. And Fradique, showing emotion (because these questions about form upset his calm), babbled that in prose he wanted "something crystalline, velvety, wavy, marbled, which all by itself could produce an absolute beauty in a plastic way and which as expression, as speech, could translate everything, from the most fugitive tones of light to the most subtle state of the soul . . ."

"In short," I exclaimed, "a prose such as there never can be!"

"No!" Fradique shouted, "*a prose such as there hasn't been yet!*"

Then he added in conclusion, "And since there isn't any yet, it's useless to write. Only forms with no beauty can be produced, and in these forms only half of what is trying to be said is expressed, because the other half is not re-ducible to words."

All this may have been specious and puerile, but it did reveal the feelings which had kept that superior being mute, possessed as he was by the sublime ambition of producing only absolutely definitive truths by means of absolutely beautiful forms.

For that reason, and not because of any Southern indolence, as Alceste in-
sinuates, Fradique passed through the world without leaving any other vestiges
of the formidable activity of his thinking self except those he spread about over
long years, like an ancient sage, "in conversations where he brought pleasure
under the plane trees of his garden or in letters that were also by nature conversations with friends separated from him by the waves . . ." His conversations
had gone with the wind, as, unlike Dr. Johnson, he had no Boswell, enthusiastic
and patient, to follow him in city and country with long attentive ears and a
pencil ready to jot down and eternalize everything. All that remains of him,
then, are his letters, the little nuggets of gold of which Alceste speaks and where
the gleam, the intrinsic value and the treasure of the rich block from which they
came can be glimpsed.

VIII

If Fradique's life was governed in that way by such a constant and clear objective
of abstention and silence, by publishing his letters I may appear to be rashly
and treacherously throwing my friend after his death into all this noise and publicity from which he had always withdrawn with a strict probity of spirit. And
that is what it would be had I not evidence that Fradique would have approved
unconditionally of the publication of his *Correspondence*, organized with judgment and love. In 1888, in a letter in which I was telling him about a romantic
trip to Brittany, I mentioned a book that I had taken along and which had
charmed me, *The Correspondence of Xavier Doudan*, one of those withdrawn
spirits who live to perfect themselves in the truth and not to glorify themselves
to the world, and who, like Fradique, have left the only vestiges of an intense
intellectual life in their correspondence, collected afterwards with reverence by
those who knew their inner thoughts.

Fradique, in the letter he sent me in reply, all full of the Pyrenees where he
had spent the summer, said in a postscript, "Doudan's correspondence is, indeed,
quite readable, even though one senses in it a naturally limited spirit who, since
youth, was rooted in the doctrinarism of the Geneva School and who later fell
into solitude and illness, knowing life, people and the world only through books.
In any case, I read those letters as I read all collections of correspondence that,
not having been didactically prepared for the public (like Pliny's), constitute an
excellent study of psychology and history. There you have a way of perpetuating

a man's ideas that I heartily approve of—by publishing his correspondence! It has, right off, this immense advantage: the value of the ideas (and therefore the choice of those which are to remain) is not decided by the one who conceived them, but by a group of friends and critics, so much freer and demanding in their judgment as they pass it on a dead man whom they only wish to show to the world through his superior and luminous sides. In addition to this, correspondence reveals the individuality of a man better than a work, and this is inestimable for those who were valued much more on earth for their character than for their talent. Furthermore, if a work doesn't always increase the wealth of human knowledge, correspondence, as it reproduces events and ways of feeling, tastes, contemporary thought, and circumstance, always necessarily enriches the treasure of historical documentation. Then, moreover, there is the fact that a man's letters, the warm and vibrant product of his life, contain more instruction than his philosophy, which is only a personal creation of his spirit. A philosophy offers merely one more conjecture to be added to the huge pile of conjectures. A life that reveals itself makes up the study of a human reality, which, placed alongside other studies, broadens our knowledge of man, the only objective *accessible* to intellectual effort. And, finally, since *letters are written lectures* (as I'm not sure which classical writer states), they have no need for the sacramental dressing as *such prose as has no equal* . . . But this point would need to be developed some more and I can hear the horse on whom I am going to ride up to Bigorre Peak stopping at the door."

It was the memory of this opinion of Fradique's, so clear and well-founded, that made me decide, as soon as the nostalgia for that beloved comrade subsided in me, to gather together his letters so that men could learn a few things and love that intelligence which I so intimately loved and followed. I devoted a year to this tender task, because Fradique's correspondence, which, with the quiet habits that sheltered that "wanderer of continents" after 1880, was the most preferred of his activities, contains the breadth and the volume of the correspondence of Cicero, Voltaire, Proudhon, and other powerful fomenters of ideas.

One can immediately feel the pleasure with which he composed these letters by the type of paper, splendid and a bit ivory-colored Whatman stock, so that his pen would run easily across the page, just as his voice would cut across the air; broad enough to contain the development of the most complex idea and strong enough in its parchment-like consistency so that the ravages of time would not prevail. "I have already calculated with Smith's help (he informs Carlos Mayer) that every one of my letters on this paper, with envelope and stamp, costs me 250 réis. Now, let us suppose with vanity that one in every five hundred of my letters contains an idea, and then it will turn out that every idea costs me *one hundred and twenty-five mil-réis*. This simple calculation should be enough for the state and the economical middle class that runs it to oppose education with ardor, since it gives incontrovertible proof that smoking is cheaper than thinking . . . I am counterbalancing *smoking* and *thinking* because they are, my dear Carlos, two identical operations which consist in giving off small puffs into the wind."

All these expensive pages have Fradique's initials—F. M.—tiny and simple, in scarlet enamel, in one corner. The writing that fills them, singularly uneven, had a fine resemblance to Fradique's conversation: now tight and narrow, seeming to bite into the paper like a chisel in order to outline the idea quite rigorously; now hesitant and slow, scratching out words and leaving gaps, like that effort of his to feel things out, to peek into and circle about their true reality; now more fluid and rapid, set down with ease and breadth, recalling those moments of abundance and inspiration which Fontan de Carmanges called *le dégel de Fradique*, and where the strait and sober expression would open up like a pennant flying in the wind.

Fradique never dated his letters and, if they were coming from dwellings familiar to his friends, he gave only the city and month. There exist, therefore, ever so many letters with the short indication: *Paris, July; Lisbon, February* . . . He would also frequently restore to the months the naturalist names of the Republican calendar: *Paris, Floreal; London, Nivose*. When he was writing to women, he would substitute for the name of the month that of the flower that best symbolized it, and I still have letters with such bucolic dates: *Florence, first violets* (which indicates the end of February); *London, arrival of the chrysanthemums* (which indicates the beginning of September). A letter from Lisbon even offers this awful date: *Lisbon, first flow of parliamentary logorrhea!* (which reveals a sad, muddy January, cabs on the Largo de São Bento, and in the building above licentiates belching out, among insults, the excreta of their old textbooks).

It is impossible, therefore, to organize Fradique's *Correspondence* in any chronological order, nor would such an order matter, given that I am not editing his complete and integral correspondence to form a continuous and intimate history of his ideas. In letters that are not those of an *author* and which do not constitute, like those of Voltaire or Proudhon, a flowing and constant commentary that accompanies and illuminates his work, it is quite proper above all to let the pages that best reveal his personality stand out, the collection of ideas, tastes, and habits, by which one can tangibly touch and feel the man. So, therefore, out of these heavy bundles of Fradique's letters, I have chosen only a few scattered ones from among those that show traces of character and glimpses of his active existence; those that afford a glimpse into some instructive episode of his life of the heart; those through which, as they ponder general notions concerning literature, art, society, and customs, the makeup of his thought can be characterized; and finally, for the special interest that sets them apart, those that refer to Portuguese matters, like his "impressions of Lisbon," transcribed with such malicious reality for the enjoyment of Madame de Jouarre.

It would of course be useless in these fragmentary pages to look for Fradique's high and free-flowing thought or his so deep and certain wisdom. In the correspondence of Fradique Mendes, as Alceste finally says, *C'est son génie qui mousse.*[20] In it we really only see the radiant and ephemeral froth that has boiled over, while lying beneath is the rich and heady wine that was never poured or served to thirsting souls. But, idly scattered about like this, it still shows in excellent relief the image of this superbly interesting man in all his manifestations of thought, passion, sociability, and action.

In addition to the desire that my contemporaries should come to love this spirit that I loved so much, by publishing the letters of Fradique Mendes I am obeying an intention of pure and certain patriotism.

A nation only lives because it thinks. *Cogitat ergo est.*[21] Power and wealth are not enough to prove that a nation lives a life that deserves to be glorified in history, the same as strong muscles and a pocketful of gold are not enough for a man to be an honor to Humanity. A kingdom in Africa, with countless warriors in its fortified aringas and countless diamonds in its hills, will always be a wild and dead land, which, for the profit of civilization, civilized peoples tread on and cut up as boldly as one butchers the dumb animal in order to nourish the thinking animal. And yet, on the other hand, if Egypt or Tunis became independent centers of science, literature, and art, and with a serene legion of geniuses educated the world incessantly, no nation, even in this age of force and iron, would dare occupy, as they would an ownerless wasteland, those august lands where a sublime flock of ideas and forms was bred for the betterment of mankind.

In truth, only thought and its supreme creations—science, literature, and art—give greatness to peoples, attract universal reverence and love for them, and, by shaping the treasure of truths and beauties that the world needs within them, make them sacrosanct before the world. What difference is there, really, between Paris and Chicago? They are two pulsating and productive cities where the palaces, institutions, parks, and wealth are superbly equivalent. So why then does Paris form a crackling hearth of civilization, with an irresistible fascination for humanity, and why Chicago and its land have only the value of a crude but formidable granary where flour and seed are sought? Because Paris, in addition to the palaces, institutions, and wealth, which Chicago can also rightly take pride in, possesses in addition a special group of men—Renan, Taine, Berthelot, Coppé, Bonnat, Falguière, Gounod, Massenet—who, by the incessant productivity of their brains, convert the banal city they inhabit into a center of sovereign learning. If *The Origins of Christianity*, *Faust*, the canvases of Bonnat, the marbles of Falguière came to us from overseas, from the new and monumental Chicago, the spirits and hearts of the earth would be turned toward Chicago and not Paris, the way plants turn toward the sun.

If a nation, therefore, is only superior because it has thought, anyone who reveals in our homeland a new man with original thought adds in a patriotic way to the greatness that will make it respected, the only beauty that will make it loved, and he will be like someone who has added one more shrine to its temples or has erected one more castle above its walls.

Michelet wrote in a letter one day, with reference to Antero de Quental, "If there are left in Portugal four or five men like the author of the *Modern Odes*, Portugal continues to be a great living country . . ." The master of *The History of France* meant that as long as it lives beside intelligence, even though it may lie dead beside action, our homeland is not completely a corpse that can be trod on and sliced up. Even though there are diverse manifestations of thought and although the same splendor doesn't gleam in all of them, they all prove the same vitality. A book of poetry can sublimely show that the soul of a nation still lives through poetical genius, a compendium of redeeming laws that emanate from a positive spirit are solid proof that a people is still alive through its political genius, but the revelation of a spirit like that of Fradique ensures that a country also lives through its least grandiose yet still worthy sides, with grace, lively invention, transcendent irony, imagination, humor, and taste . . .

In the uncertain and bitter times we live in, such Portuguese cannot remain forever forgotten, far away, under the silence of a mute marble slab. Therefore, I am revealing Fradique to my fellow citizens—as a consolation and a hope.

The Letters

To the Viscount de A.T.
LONDON, MAY

My dear countryman,

Only late yesterday evening, when I returned from the country, did I find your note with which you did me considerable honor by asking about my experience as to "Who is the best tailor in London?" That depends entirely on what your needs for that artist might be. If you are only seeking a man who can cover your nudity comfortably and with economy, I recommend the one whose shop is closest to your hotel. There are all those steps to be saved and, as Ecclesiastes says, every step shortens the distance to the tomb.

If, however, my dear countryman, you wish a tailor who will give you consideration and standing in your world, whom you can name with pride at the door of the Havanesa, turning about slowly to display the flow and fine cut of the waist, which will enable you to mention the names of the Lords you met there, who with the tips of their canes were picking out from the racks up above cheviots for hunting jackets, and which will serve you later in old age, at the hunchbacked time of rheumatism, as a consoling memory of youthful elegance, then with strong insistence I must recommend Cook (Thomas Cook), who is the very latest fashion, absolutely ruinous, and gets everything wrong.

For any subsequent advice on "suppliers," in London or elsewhere in the Universe, remaining always at your pleasure and for your service is

Fradique Mendes

II

To Madame de Jouarre
(Transl.)*

Dear Godmother,

Yesterday at Madame de Tressan's, as I passed by escorting Libuska to dinner, seated next to you chatting under the atrocious portrait of Marshal de Mouy's wife was a blonde lady with a high, pale forehead who immediately seduced me, perhaps because I could sense, in spite of her being indolently buried in a divan, a rare grace in her walk, the proud and light grace of a goddess or a bird. Quite different from our wise Libuska, who moves with the splendid weight of a statue! And from an interest in that other step, possibly winged and *Dianic* (as in Diana), come these scribblings.

Who was she? I expect she came to us from the deepest countryside, from some old castle in Anjou with weeds in its moat, because I don't remember ever having come across in Paris that fabulously golden hair, like the December sun in London, those sad and sloping *angelic* shoulders, in imitation of a Madonna by Mantegna, and so absolutely rare in France ever since the reign of Charles X, the time of misunderstood hearts and Balzac's *Lily of the Valley*. I could not admire with equal fervor her black dress, dominated by scandalously yellow details. Her arms were perfect, though, and from her lashes, when she lowered them, a sad romance seemed to hang. In that way she gave me a first impression of a plaintive maiden from the time of Chateaubriand. In her eyes, however, later on, I caught a spark of perceptible vivacity that dated her more as from the eighteenth century. You are probably asking, my Godmother, "How could I take in so much as I strolled past, with Libuska beside me checking things?" The fact is that I turned. I turned and from the doorway I admired once more the plaintive shoulders of the thirteenth-century Virgin, her mass of hair that bunched candles among the orchids behind her touched with gold, and, most of all, the subtle enchantment of her eyes, her delicate and languid eyes . . . *Delicate and languid eyes.* That's the first expression I have today that decently captures reality.

Why didn't I move things farther along and ask for an "introduction"? I really don't know. Maybe the refinement of *postponing*, which led La Fontaine always to choose the longest path as he headed toward happiness. Do you know

---

*[Note in the original] Many of the letters of Fradique Mendes published here were naturally written in French. All these are accompanied by the abbreviation Transl. (translated).

what gave such seduction to the fairies' palace in the time of King Arthur? You don't. That's what comes of not reading Tennyson . . . Well, it was the immense number of years it took to get there, through enchanted gardens where every corner of the forest offered the unexpected emotion of a flirtation, a battle or a banquet . . . (With what morbid propensity did I wake up today for Asiatic style!) As a matter of fact, after my contemplation in the doorway, I went back to take supper alongside my radiant tyrant. But between the banal *foie-gras* sandwich and a glass of Tokay, not at all like the Tokay that Voltaire, old already, recalled having drunk at the home of Madame d'Étoiles (the wines of the Tressans descend in a male line from the poisons of Brinvilliers), I kept seeing, *I saw*, those *delicate and languid eyes*. Only man among the animals would mingle the languor of a delicate look with slices of *foie-gras*. A thoroughbred dog certainly wouldn't. But would we have been desired by the "ephemeral feminine" were it not for that providential bestiality? Only the portion of matter that there is in a man makes women resign themselves to the incorrigible portion of the ideal there is in him too—for the eternal perturbation of the world. What prejudiced Petrarch most in Laura's eyes was his sonnets. And when Romeo, with one foot already on the silken ladder, lingered, exhaling his ecstasies in invocations to the night and the moon, Juliet was tapping her impatient fingers on the edge of the balcony and thinking, "Oh, isn't that son of the Montagues the gabby one!" This detail isn't noted in Shakespeare, but it has been proven all through the Renaissance. Don't chide me for this sincerity of a Southern skeptic and let me know the name in your parish of the blonde chatelaine from Anjou. Speaking of castles, letters from Portugal tell me that the gazebo I had built at my country place in Sintra, and which was meant for you as "your place for thinking and retreat at siesta time," has collapsed. Thirty-eight hundred damned francs gone to waste. Everything goes to ruin in a country that's all ruins. The architect who built it is a Deputy and he writes financial news articles in the *Jornal da Tarde*. My lawyer in Sintra advises me to rebuild the gazebo with the services of a fine young fellow from a good family who understands construction and works in the State's Attorney's office. Maybe if I needed some legal advice he would recommend a stone mason. These are the jolly elements with which we're trying to restore our empire in Africa!

Your humble and devoted servant,

Fradique

III

To Oliveira Martins
PARIS, MAY

Dear friend,

I am finally fulfilling the promise made in your erudite hermitage of Águas Férreas on that beautiful March morning when we were chatting in the sun about the character of the ancients—I am sending you, as documentation, the photograph of the mummy of Ramses II (which the banal Frenchman, following the banal Greek, has insisted on calling Sesostris), recently discovered by Professor Maspero in the royal sarcophagi of Medinet-Abu.

My dear Oliveira Martins, don't you find this fact roguishly suggestive—*Ramses photographed*? . . . But precisely there we find the justification for the mummification of corpses, as done by the good Egyptians with such effort and expense, so that men might enjoy in their earthly form what the Scribe calls "the benefits of eternity." Ramses, as he believed, and of which he was assured by the metaphysicians of Thebes, rises up again "with all the bones and skin that were his" in this year of Our Lord 1886. And 1886, for a Pharaoh of the Nineteenth Dynasty, fourteen hundred years before Christ, quite decently represents *Eternity* and *Future Life*. So here we are now, able to gaze upon the "true features" of the greatest of the Ramesides, as real as he was for Hokem, his chief eunuch, or Pentaur, his chief chronicler, or those who in olden times, on days of triumph, would run to spread flowers in his path "wearing their festive wigs and with their skin anointed with Segabai oil." There you have him now, in a photograph, eyes closed and smiling. And what will you tell me about the royal face? What humbling reflections on the irremediable degeneration of man does it bring on! Where is there today among those who govern people anyone who has that sovereign face of calm and immeasurable pride, that superior smile of omnipotent benevolence, of an ineffable benevolence that takes in the whole world, that air of unperturbed and unconquerable strength, all that virile splendor that three thousand years in the darkness of a catacomb could not extinguish? There you have a true *Master of Men*! Compare that august countenance with the sluggish, recessive, and mustachioed profile of a Napoleon III, with the chained bulldog's snout of a Bismarck, with the pudding face of the Russian Tsar, a spiritless and affable fat face that could be that of his head waiter. Such shallowness, such grubby ugliness in those faces of the powerful!

Where does this come from? The soul is the model for the face, just as the breath of the ancient potter modeled the fine vase, and in our cultures today there is no place for a soul to be certain of itself and thus produce itself in an absolute expansion of its strength. In olden times a simple man, a bundle of muscles on a bundle of bones, could rise up and work like an element of nature. All that was needed was the unlimited desire to draw unlimited power from it. There we have in Ramses someone who can want everything and can do everything and to whom Ptah, the wise god, says with great awe, "Your will gives life and your will gives death!" He drives along races as he pleases, north, south, and east. He changes and destroys the frontiers of kingdoms like fences in a field; new cities rise up in his footsteps; all the fruits of the earth are for him and all the hopes of men turn to him; the place upon which he casts gaze is blessed and prospers and the place that does not receive that beneficent light lies like "the clod of earth unkissed by the Nile"; the gods depend on him and Amon trembles uneasily when before the pillars of his temple Ramses cracks the three twisted strands of his whip of war! There you have a man, and one who can most surely claim in his triumphal song, "Everything bows to my strength, I go and I come with the swift steps of a lion, the king of the gods sits to my right and to my left. When I speak, Heaven listens, earthly things lie down at my feet so that I may pluck them with a free hand, and I am forever raised up over the throne of the earth!"

"The earth," of course, was that region, sandy for the most part, that extends from the Libyan mountains to Mesopotamia, and there has never been a more petulant panegyric than that of the scribes. But the man is, or believes himself to be, just that great. And this awareness of greatness, of unlimited power, shines necessarily in his features and provides that proud majesty, fraught with smiling serenity, that Ramses has kept intact even beyond life, dried up, mummified and stuffed with mineral pitch from Judaea.

On the other hand, just take a look at the conditions that surround a powerful person like Bismarck today. A poor devil like that stands above nothing and depends on everything. Every impulse of his will runs up against the resistance of some obstacle. His action in the world is a perpetual beating of his skull against the thickness of some well-defended doors. All manner of conventions, traditions, laws, doctrines, interests, and principles rise up at every turn before his steps like sacred markers. An article in the newspaper makes him stop, hesitate. The pettifoggery of a legalist obliges him to withdraw hurriedly the claw that he had been extending. Ten plump bourgeois and ten long-haired professors voting in a chamber can demolish the high scaffolding of his plans. A few florins in a bag become the torment of his nights. It is as impossible for him to dispose of a citizen as of a star. He can never take a leap forward, erect and sure of himself, it must be one that weaves and sniffs things out. His watchful surroundings impose on him the basic necessity of speaking softly and secretly instead of "plucking earthly things with a free hand," so he pilfers their crumbs after some dark intrigues. The irresistible currents of ideas, sentiments, and interests work beneath him, around him, and, although seemingly directing them with much waving of arms and shouting from up on high, he is really being dragged along by them. In just that way an all-powerful person of Bismarck's type sometimes moves along with the appearance of being on top of great events but, like a loose buoy, he goes carried along on top of the current.

Miserable omnipotence! And the feeling of that wretchedness cannot help but affect the features of our powerful ones, giving them that constricted look, tight, tortured, sour, and, above all, *forced*, as can be seen on the faces of Napoleon, the Tsar, Bismarck, all of those who gather together the greatest amount of contemporary power, the *forced* look of something that rolls along to meet up with things by bumping against walls.

In conclusion, let me say that Ramses II's mummy (the only authentic face of an ancient man we know) proves that with the impossibility of human life being lived in its fullest freedom and fullest strength, with no other limits but those of its own desires, what has been lost forever along with the physical shape of the man is the highest and perfect expression of greatness. There is no longer a sublime face, only pasty, ugly faces where bile carves wrinkles along the folds of the skin. The only noble features are those of the wild beasts, genuine Ramseses in their wilderness, having lost nothing of their strength or their freedom. Modern man, that fellow, even at his social height, is a poor Adam crushed between two pages of a law.

If you find all this excessive and fantasizing, you may attribute it to the fact that I have dined and inevitably conversed with your coreligionary P., a State's Attorney and *muchas cosas más*, as the Spanish say, many other things, although the *más* could well be Portuguese in its meaning of very bad things. This letter, then, is the violent reaction to that lawyerly and lawyerish conversation. Ah, my friend, my unfortunate friend, what do you do after receiving the labial flow of a counselor? I give myself an inner bath—a purifying bath, an immense bath of fantasy, wherein I decant, as an incorrupt perfume, a flask of Shelley or Musset.

Your true friend *et nunc et semper*,[22]

Fradique Mendes

IV

To Madame S.

PARIS, FEBRUARY

My dear friend,

The name of the Spaniard is Don Ramón Covarubia. He lives at 12 Passage Saulnier, and as he is Aragonese and therefore frugal, I think that he would be quite happy with ten francs a lesson. But if your son already knows enough Castilian to understand the Romanceros, *Don Quixote*, some picaresque novels, twenty pages of Quevedo, a couple of plays by Lope de Vega, a novel or two of Galdós, which is enough of the literature of Spain for him to read, why should you, my sensible friend, wish him to pronounce the Castilian that he knows with the accent, the savor, and the spark of a native of Madrid born out of the very stones of the Calle Mayor? Is this how young Raul is going to waste the time that society has marked out for him to acquire ideas and perceptions (and society, for a lad of his wealth and name and good looks, grants only seven years for that intellectual nourishment, from the age of eleven to that of eighteen), doing what? In the luxury of honing the mere instrument for the acquisition of ideas and perceptions to a superfine and superfluous perfection? Because languages, my good friend, are only tools of knowledge, working tools. Using energy and life in learning to pronounce them so purely and so genuinely that one would appear to have been born within them and to have called, in each and every one of them, for life's first bread and water, is to act like a farmer who, instead of being satisfied with a plain iron hoe on a plain wooden handle, would spend months, when his garden should be worked, at carving emblems on the metal and flowers and leaves up and down the handle. With such a gardener, so minutely occupied in embellishing and beautifying his hoe, in what state, my dear lady, would your Touraine orchards be now?

A man should only speak with impeccable assurance and purity the language of his own country; all the others he should speak poorly, poorly but proudly, with the flat and false accent that immediately marks him as a foreigner. Nationality truly resides in language, and whoever goes about possessing with growing perfection the languages of Europe will gradually experience a denationalization. He will no longer have the special and exclusive enchantment of his *mother tongue*, be enwrapped in its affective influences, which separate him from other races, and the cosmopolitanism of language will irremediably give him a cosmopolitanism of character. That's why a polyglot is never a patriot. With every alien language he assimilates into his moral organism alien ways of thinking are introduced, alien ways of feeling. His patriotism disappears, diluted by foreign-ness. *Rue de Rivoli, Calle de Alcalá, Regent Street, Wilhelmstrasse*, what difference does it make to him? They're all streets, paved with stone or macadam. In all of them the speech around him offers natural and like element where his spirit moves freely, spontaneously, without hesitation, without friction. And since it is with speech, which is the essential instrument for blending, he can blend with all of them, it is in all of them that he feels and accepts a mother country.

On the other hand, the continued efforts of a man to express himself with genuine and exact propriety in construction and accent of foreign languages, that is, the effort to blend with foreign peoples in what they have as essentially characteristic, speech, suppresses in him all native individuality. After many years, this skilled practitioner who has come to speak other languages than his own absolutely well will have lost all originality of spirit, because his ideas must necessarily have the uncharacteristic and neutral nature that allows them to be indifferently adapted to languages that are the most opposite in character and temperament. They must, in fact, be like those "bodies of wretches" that the country folk speak of so sadly, "who would fit into the clothes of anybody and everybody."

In addition, the idea of pronouncing foreign languages with perfection makes for a lamentable fawning toward the foreigner. Regarding him there is something like a servile desire not to be ourselves, of our blending in with him in what he has that is most his, that belongs most to him, his language. So this is an abdication of national dignity. No, my dear lady! Let us speak the languages of others nobly and poorly, patriotically poorly. If only because the polyglot inspires mistrust in foreigners as someone who has no roots or stable home, someone who rolls along through foreign nationalities, successively disguising himself in them, and tries to build a life in all of them, because in none of them is he tolerated. As a matter of fact, my dear friend, if you were to thumb through court records you would see that perfect polyglotism is an instrument of high *escroquerie*.

But here you have me carried away by dilettantism! Instead of an address I give you a treatise! . . . I hope my garrulousness has at least made you smile, think, and save our poor Raul the dreary chore of pronouncing *Viva la Gracia*! and *Benditos sean tus ojos*! as exactly as if he were living on a corner of the Puerta del Sol, wearing a cape with velvet fringe, sucking on a *lazarillo* cigarette. This, however, should not stop you from using Don Ramón's services. In addition to being a disciple of Zorrilla he is a guitarist, and he can replace lessons in the language of Quevedo with lessons in the guitar of Almaviva. Your handsome

Raul will even pick up in that way a new faculty of expression, the faculty of expressing emotions by means of wire cords. And this gift, my good friend, is an excellent one! It is much better in youth, and even in old age, to learn how, through the strings of a guitar, to unburden the soul of confused and nameless things that are swirling about in it than to be able, along stopovers in the way stations of the world, to ask with perfection for some bread and cheese in Swedish, Dutch, Greek, Bulgarian, and Polish.

And is that really necessary, even in order to provide him throughout the world with those vital necessities of stomach and soul, this threshing over the years by the harsh hand of teachers of "the sloughs and deserts of grammar and pronunciation," as old Milton said? I had an admirable aunt who spoke only Portuguese (or, rather, the Minho dialect) and who traveled all over Europe with ease and comfort. That lady, smiling but dyspeptic, ate only eggs, which she knew only by their national and vernacular name, *ovos*. For her, *huevos, oeufs, eggs, das Ei* were sounds of raw nature, not very distinguishable from the croaking of frogs or the crackle of firewood. So, when in London, Berlin, Paris, or Moscow, if she wanted her eggs, this expeditious woman would call over the waiter, fix her sharp and meaningful eyes on him, and squat gravely on the carpet and imitate, with a slow puffing up of her ample skirts, a hen in the act of laying as she shouted *cluck-cluck-cluck, cluck-cluck-cluck*! In no intelligent city or religion in the Universe did my aunt not have her eggs to eat, and they were superbly fresh!

I kiss the hand of my kind friend,

Fradique

V

To Guerra Junqueiro

PARIS, MAY

My dear friend,

Your letter overflows with poetical illusion. To suppose, as you innocently do, that by using poetry (even yours, sharper and more sparkling than the arrows of Apollo) to skewer church priests, sacristies, Friday fast, and the bones of martyrs you can "cleanse God of the avalanche of priestly rubbish" and elevate the people (among people you must certainly be including counselors of state) to a completely pure and abstract understanding of religion, a religion that consists only of a morality that rests on a faith, is to have a dreamy notion of religion, its essence, and its object, a notion of a dreamer who persists in his dreams.

My good friend, a religion from which ritual has been eliminated will disappear, because for mankind (with the exception of some few metaphysicians, moralists, and mystics) religions are nothing but an agglomeration of rites by which every people tries to establish communication with its God and obtain favors from him. This and only this is the end of all cults, from the earliest, the cult of Indra, to the recent cult of the Heart of Mary, which has scandalized you so much in your parish, you incorrigibly devout adept of idealism!

If you wish to verify this historically, leave Viana do Castelo, take a walking stick, and climb with me through the antiquity outside there to a well-cultivated and well-watered place that lies between the Indus River, the Himalayan cliffs, and the sands of a great desert. Here we are in Septa Sindhu, in the land of the Seven Waters, in the Happy Valley, in the land of the Aryans. In the first village where we stop you will see, up on a knoll, a stone altar covered with cool moss, on top of which a slow fire is burning with a pale light and men dressed in linen are moving about around it, their long hair held in rings of fine gold. They are priests, my friend! They are the first chaplains of humanity and all of them on this hot May dawn are celebrating a right of the Aryan mass. One of them is cleaning and pruning the wood that will nourish the sacred fire. Another is pounding in a mortar, with blows that sound like the drumbeats of victory, the aromatic herbs that go into the making of Soma. That one there, like a sower, is scattering oats around the altar; another beside him is lifting his open palms to heaven and intoning an austere chant. These men, my friend, are performing a rite that contains within itself the whole religion of the Aryans, one which has as its object the propitiation of Indra: Indra, the Sun, Fire, the divine power that can fill the heart of Aria with ruination and grief by sucking up the water of the irrigation ditches, burning the grazing lands, unleashing pestilence into ponds, turning Septa Sindhu more sterile than the "heart of the Evil One"; or it can melt the snows of the Himalayas and, with a thunderbolt, release "the rain that lives in the belly of the clouds," giving the rivers back their waters, the fields their greenness, the ponds their health, and joy and plenty to the dwellings of Aria. It is therefore simply a matter of convincing Indra, always propitious, to pour down upon Septa Sindhu all the favors that a rural pastoral people might desire.

There are no metaphysics here, no ethics, nor are there any explanations of the nature of the gods or rules for the conduct of men. There is only a liturgy, a totality of the rite that Aria must observe if Indra is to listen to them, because all through the experience of generations it has been proven that Indra will only listen to them and only grant the favors they ask for when certain old men of a certain caste, dressed in white linen, lift up their voices in sweet chants to him around his altar and offer up libations, gathering together gifts of fruits, honey, and the flesh of lambs. Without gifts, without libations, without chants, without lamb, Indra, sulking and withdrawn into the depths of the invisible and the intangible, will not descend to earth and spread his bounty. And if a poet were to come from Viana do Castelo and take away from Aria its moss-covered altar, its sacred firewood, its mortar, its strainer, and its cup of Soma, Aria would be left without the means for propitiating its God, be out of touch with its God, and it will be left on earth like a small child with no one to feed it and no one to watch over its steps.

This primordial religion is the absolute and unchanging form of religion, one that all instinctively repeat and in which (in spite of the alien elements of theology, metaphysics, and ethics that superior minds have introduced into it) they are ultimately as one in reverence. In all climes and among all races, with either giving divinity to the forces of nature or to the souls of the dead, religions, my friend, are always really made up of a set of practices by means of which a simple man can seek through the friendship of God the supreme possessions of health, strength, peace, and bounty. And even now when, believing in his own efforts, he asks for these possessions through hygiene, order, law, and work, he still persists in performing propitiable rites so that God will aid his efforts.

What you have observed in Septa Sindhu you will also be able to verify in like manner (before retiring to Viana to drink that *vinho verde* of Monção, of which you have written so many dithyrambs) by pausing in classical antiquity, in Athens or Rome, wherever you wish, in the moment of the greatest splendor and culture of Greco-Latin civilizations. If you ask an ancient there, whether a potter from Suburra or the Flamen Dialis himself, what the body of doctrines and moral concepts that make up religion consists of, he will smile, not understanding. And he will reply that religion consists of *paces deorum quaerere*, of pacifying the gods, of assuring the benevolence of the gods. In the mind of the ancients that means fulfilling the rites, the practices, the formulas, that long tradition has shown to be the only ones that will succeed in catching the attention of the gods and persuading and seducing them. And it was indispensible in that ceremony not to alter the value of a single syllable or the value of a gesture in the sacrifice because, otherwise, the god, not recognizing the sacrifice he prefers or the prayer that pleases him, would remain inattentive and alien and the religion would be falsifying its supreme end, to influence the god. Worse still, it would appear as a negation of religion, and the god, seeing that omission in the liturgy as a lack of reverence, would immediately dispatch the barbs of his wrath from on high. The slant of the folds in the robe of the sacrificer, a step to the right or a movement to the left, the slow dripping of the libation, the size of the logs for the votive flames, all these details had been immutably prescribed for the rites and their exclusion or alteration constituted impiety. It also constituted a true crime against the nation, because it brought down the indignation of the gods upon it. How many legions were defeated, how many fortresses demolished because a priest let drop a grain of ash from the altar or because the augurer neglected to pull enough wool from the head of the lamb? That was why Athens would punish a priest who altered the ceremony and the Senate would depose consuls who made a mistake in the sacrifice, even something as minor as keeping the edge of his toga over his head when he should have let it slip down to his shoulder. So that in Rome, if you composed preciously ironic verses about a divinity you could be a great and admired comic poet, but if you satirized the liturgy and rites, as you do in *The Old Age of the Eternal Father*, you became a public enemy, a traitor to the state, condemned to the Tulian dungeons.

And if, having had enough of those ancient times, you wish to return to our own philosophical days, you will find in the two great religions of West and East, Catholicism and Buddhism, an even more salient and living proof that religion basically consists of practices, on top of which theology and morality have been superimposed without penetrating them, simply as an intellectual luxury, complementary and transitory: flowers placed on the altar by the imagination or by idealistic virtue. Catholicism (no one knows it more fervently than you) is today summed up in short series of material observances and, yet, there has never been a religion in which intelligence has erected a vaster and higher structure of theological and moral concepts. Those concepts, however, the work of scholars and mystics, never really left the schools and monasteries where they were the valuable material for dialectics or poetry. They never penetrated the multitudes to methodically govern their judgments or to consciously govern their actions. Reduced to catechisms and primers, that body of concepts was learned by heart by the people, but the people were never persuaded that they were living religiously, and that therefore they *pleased God* and *served God*, if they just fulfilled the Ten Commandments, outside of all ritual practice and observance. And they only learned those Ten Commandments and the Good Works and other moral precepts of the catechism by heart with the idea that those versicles, *recited with the lips,* had a miraculous virtue of being able to attract the attention, good will, and favors of the Lord. To *serve God*, which is the way to *please God*, the essential thing was always to hear mass, say the rosary, fast, take communion, make promises, donate robes to the saints, etc. Only through these rituals and not through the moral fulfillment of moral laws is God propitiated, and only thus can one obtain from him the inestimable gifts of health, happiness, wealth, and peace. Heaven and hell themselves, the extraterrestrial reward or punishment by the Law, was never gained or avoided in the minds of the people through a punctual fulfillment of the Law. And, rightfully perhaps, for that very reason in Catholicism rewards and punishments are not manifestations of God's *justice* but of God's *grace*. Grace, now, in the thoughts of simple people can only be obtained through the constant and tireless practice of the precepts: mass, fasting, penance, communion, rosary, novenas, offerings, and promises. So that in the Catholicism of the inhabitants of Minho, just as in the religion of the Aryans, the same in Septa Sindhu as in Carrazeda de Ansiães, everything can be summed up in propitiating God by means of practices that are pleasing to him. There is no theology here, there are no morals. There is the act of the infinitely weak wishing to please the infinitely strong. And if you try to purify this Catholicism by eliminating priests, stoles, wafers, and holy water, all the ritual and all the liturgy, a Catholic will immediately abandon a religion that has no visible church and doesn't offer him the simple and tangible means of communicating with God, of receiving from him transcendental rewards for his soul and perceptible rewards for his body. Catholicism will have ended at that instant; millions of people will have lost their God. The church is the vessel, with God as its perfume. With the church gone, God will have evaporated.

If we had the time to go to China or Ceylon, you would come across the same phenomenon in Buddhism. That religion has elaborated the highest form of metaphysics, the noblest of moral codes, but in all the races it has penetrated, from the most barbarous to the most cultivated, from the hordes of Nepal to the Mandarin realm of China, for the multitudes it has always consisted of rites, ceremonies, and practices, the best known of which is the *prayer wheel*. Have you ever encountered that wheel? It is distressingly similar to a coffee mill. You will see it in all Buddhist countries, placed on city streets and on rural crossroads, so that the devout, when they pass, can give the handle a couple of turns and make the prayers written inside chime, communicating in this way with the Buddha who, by means of this transcendental courtesy, "will be thankful and will increase their bounty."

Neither Catholicism nor Buddhism is because of this headed for decline. Quite the contrary! They stand in their natural and normal state of religion. The more a religion becomes material the more popular it becomes and, therefore, the more divine it becomes. You mustn't be startled. What I mean is that the more it rids itself of its intellectual elements of theology, morality, humanitarianism, etc., driving them off to their natural regions, which are philosophy, ethics, and poetry, the more it brings the people face to face with their God in a direct and simple union, which is so easy to bring about that with a mere bending of knees, a mere mumbling of Pater Nosters, the Absolute Man who is in heaven comes to meet the transitory man who is on earth. And, since this meeting is the essentially divine core of religion, the more material it becomes the more truly divine is religion capable of becoming.

But you will no doubt say (and, in fact, you have said it), "Let us make this communication purely spiritual and thus, stripped of all liturgical externality, it will be something like the human spirit speaking to the divine spirit." But in order to have that the Millennium must come, when every digger of ditches will be a philosopher and thinker, and when that detestable Millennium arrives and every cab in the street is driven by a Mallebranche, you will still have to attach to this perfect masculine humanity a new feminine humanity, physiologically different from the one that today beautifies the earth. Because just as long as there is a woman physically, intellectually, and morally constituted like the one Jehovah, with such great artistic inspiration, made out of Adam's rib, there will always be alongside her, for the use of her weakness, an altar, an image, and a priest.

This mystical communion between man and God that you want can never be anything but the privilege of a deplorably limited spiritual elite. For the vast mass of humanity in all ages, pagan, Buddhist, Christian, Muslim, savage or civilized, religion will always have as an end, as its essence the supplication of divine favors and the avoidance of divine wrath, and as a material instrumentation to bring these objectives about, churches, priests, altars, rites, vestments, and images. Pick any average man of the crowd (as long as he's not a philosopher, a moralist, or a mystic) and ask him what religion is. An Englishman will say: "It is going well-dressed to services on Sunday to sing hymns." The Hindu will say: "It's performing *poojah* every day and paying tribute to the Mahadeo." The African will say: "It's offering up to the Mulungu his ration of flour and oil." The man from Minho will say: "It's hearing mass, reciting the rosary, fasting on Fridays, and receiving communion on Easter." And they will all be overwhelmingly right, because their objective as religious creatures is all a matter of communicating with God, and those are the means of communication with which their respective states of civilization and the respective liturgies that emerged from the latter have equipped them. *Voilà!* For you, of course, and for other chosen spirits, religion is something else, just as it was already in Athens for Socrates and in Rome for Seneca. But the masses of humanity are not made up of Socrateses and Senecas, fortunately for them and for those who govern them, including you, who would like to govern them.

Don't be disconsolate in the end, my friend. Even among simple people there are ways of being religious that are completely stripped of liturgy and ritual externalities. One form that I witnessed was delightfully pure and intimate. It was on the banks of the Zambezi. A black chieftain, Lubenga by name, on the eve of going to war with a neighboring chief wanted to communicate with his God, with his Mulungu (who was, as always, an ancestor of his made divine). The message, or request, that he wished to send to his divinity could not be transmitted through the witch doctors and their ritual, so grave and confidential were the matters it contained . . . What did Lubenga do? He shouted for a slave, passed on the message, slowly and with pauses, into his ear. He made sure that the slave had understood everything, retained everything, then he immediately seized an ax and cut off the slave's head, calmly shouting, "Go!" The soul of the slave had departed, like a letter sealed with wax and stamped, straight to heaven and to the Mulungu. But an instant later the chief slapped his forehead and quickly called another slave, whispered some quick words into his ear, picked up the axe, and lopped off his head, shouting: "Go!"

He'd forgotten some detail in his request to the Mulungu . . . The second slave was a postscript . . .

This simple manner of communicating with God ought to be dear to your heart.

A friend of the aforementioned,

Fradique

VI
To Ramalho Ortigão
PARIS, APRIL

My dear Ramalho,

Saturday afternoon, on the rue Cambon, I caught sight of our Eduardo riding in a fiacre when he stuck out his head and shouted to me: "Ramalho, tonight! On his way to Holland! Ten o'clock at the Café de la Paix!"

I became deliciously excited, and at nine-thirty, in spite of my rightful dislike of the corner by the Café de la Paix, that gaudy center of international snobbery, I installed myself there with a bock beer and waited to see the splendor of the Ramalhian countenance rise up at any moment out of the drab, limp crowd along the boulevard. At ten o'clock, leaping anxiously out of a fiacre, was the lively Carmonde, who had abandoned in haste a merry after-dinner group *pour voir ce grand Ortigan!*[23] A double wait then began, with double bocks. No sign of Ramalho or his energy. At eleven o'clock Eduardo appeared, panting. What about Ramalho? Still no word. A triple wait, triple impatience, triple bocks. And that was how we were until the bells tolled the end of the day.

As compensation there was an event, and a profound one it was. Carmonde, Eduardo, and I were sipping the dregs of our bocks, having by now given up on Ramalho and his magnificence, when, gliding by our table, there was a swarthy, skinny, rather well-dressed individual carrying in his hand respectfully, almost religiously, a superb bouquet of yellow carnations. He was a man from across the sea, from Argentina or Peru, and a friend of Eduardo, who stopped him and introduced "Mr. Mendibal." Mendibal accepted a bock and I began to make a quick study of that small face that seemed all profile, as if cut out from the blade of an ax, with the copperish hue of an English bowler hat, and where his skimpy hesitant beard, which gave witness to a faint masculinity, was something like the fuzz on a fruit, a black fuzz, not much darker than his skin. His beveled forehead drew back, in retreat, startled. The lump of his scrawny throat, on the contrary, jutted forward like the prow of a galley between the bent tips of a very high collar, shinier than enamel. There was a fat pearl on his necktie.

I contemplated and Mendibal spoke. He spoke in a laggard sort of way, almost plaintively, with the final syllables fading away and dissipating into a moan. His voice was completely disconsolate, but what it was saying conveyed a most vigorous, secure, and insolent satisfaction at being alive. That animal had everything: vast properties overseas, the respect of his suppliers, a house in Parc-Monceau, and an "adorable wife." How he slipped in mention of that lady who embellished his home I don't know. There was a moment when I got up, called over by an old English friend of mine, back from the opera and simply wishing to whisper to me with great conviction that it was "a splendid evening." When I returned to the table and to my bock, the Argentine had launched into a monologue of glorification of "his lady." Carmonde was devouring the little man with eyes that were laughing and enjoying, delightfully amused. Eduardo, that one, was listening with the heavy composure of an ancient Portuguese. And

Mendibal, having laid the bouquet of carnations on a chair with devout care, was analysing minutely the virtues and the charms of Madame. One could sense in him one of those effervescent, bubbling kinds of admiration that cannot be contained, that overflow in all directions, even over the tables in a café. Wherever he went, that man would let his adoration for his wife flow out of him, the way a soaked umbrella inevitably drips water. I understood what was at stake from the moment he revealed, his Adam's apple bulging out with pleasure, that Madame Mendibal was French. There we had the fanaticism of a black for the blonde grace of a Parisian lass, piquant in slyness and seduction. Since I understood, I sympathized. And the Argentine sniffed out in me that critical benevolence, because it was to me that he turned, unveiling the final and most decisive feature of the excellencies of Madame: "Yes, absolutely, there's no other like her in Paris! For example, the love with which she took care of Maman (his mother), a lady well on in years, loaded down with ailments! All patience, a delight, subjecting herself . . . even falling to her knees! And in recent times Maman had been so cantankerous!" Madame Mendibal had even become thinner, so he had asked her to go, as a distraction, to Versailles, where her own mother, Madame Jouffroy, lived for reasons of economy. And now he had just come from meeting her at the Saint-Lazare station. Well, gentlemen, the good creature had spent the whole day in Versailles taking care of his mother-in-law with a great longing for home, anxious to return. She didn't even enjoy the visit to her mother. The greater part of that afternoon, and such a lovely afternoon it had been, she had spent gathering that splendid bunch of yellow carnations to bring him, for him!

"It's true. Just have a look at this bouquet of carnations! It really cheers me up. Look, for small tokens like this, loving touches like this, there's no one like a Frenchwoman. Thank God I can say that I hit the bull's-eye. And if I had children, even only one, a boy, I wouldn't change places with the Prince of Wales. I don't know if you're married. Pardon my asking. But if you're not, I'm telling you what I always tell everybody: Marry a Frenchwoman, marry a Frenchwoman! . . ."

There couldn't have been anything more sincerely grotesque and touching. Since you weren't coming, flighty Ramalho, we broke up. Mendibal got into a fiacre with his loving bunch of carnations. I dragged myself along in the heat of the night over to the club. At the club I ran into Chambray, you know him, the "handsome Chambray." I found him slouching in an easy chair, worn out and radiant. I asked Chambray how life was treating him, what he thought of this day of our lives. Chambray declared that life was a delight. And immediately, without holding back, he told me the secret that had been dancing about impatiently behind his smile and his moist eyes.

He'd gone to Versailles with the intention of visiting the Fouquiers. In the same compartment with him was a woman, *une grande et belle femme*.[24] The superb body of Diana in a tight dress by Redfern. Hair parted in the middle, thick and infatuating, flowing over her short forehead. Serious eyes. Two single diamonds in her ears. A substantial, solid person, with no padding and no fakery, well-fed, well taken care of, and well set up in life.

And along with this physical and social respectability, a greedy way of continually licking her lips, briskly, with a tip of her tongue . . . Chambray thought to himself: "A bourgeoise, thirty years old, an income of sixty thousand francs, a strong temperament, disappointed in bed." And as soon as the train started he assumed his "grand Chambray manner" and pierced the lady with one of those looks that in times past had been symbolized by Cupid's arrows. Madame was impassive. But moments later, coming from between somewhat heavy eyelids, directly at Chambray (who was peeking from behind his opened *Figaro*) was one of those searching rays of light, like the ones from Diogenes's lantern, looking for a man who was a man. When they got to Courbevoie, with the pretext of lowering the window because of the dust, Chambray risked a brave but timid word about the Paris heat. She offered another, still hesitant and vague, about the coolness of the country. The eclogue had begun. In Suresnes Chambray was already sitting on the seat beside her, smoking. In Sèvres Madame's hand was grasped by Chambray, Chambray's hand was pushed away by Madame, and both became unconsciously entwined. In Viroflay there came a sudden proposal by Chambray that they take a stroll through a place in Viroflay that only he knew, a bucolic spot of incomparable loveliness, inaccessible to a bourgeois. Then, at two o'clock, they could take the next train to Versailles. And he wouldn't even let her hesitate; he caught her, morally or, rather, physiologically, by the simple strength of his warm voice, his happy eyes, and his whole open and masculine person.

There they were in the country, with an aroma of plant life all around them and springtime and Satan conspiring and blowing their warm breaths over Madame. Chambray knew a small inn by the side of the woods, at the water's edge and where the windows are entwined with woodbine. Why don't they go there for lunch, some chowder washed down with white wine from Suresnes? As a matter of fact, she does have the happy little hunger of a bird loose in the field, and, wagging his tail, Satan runs on ahead to set things up at the little inn. There they find a really magnificent arrangement: a cool, quiet room, a table all set, a linen curtain that both hides and reveals a bedroom in the rear. "In any case, have them bring lunch up right away because we have to catch the two o'clock train," was Chambray's sincere order.

When the chowder arrived, Chambray had a stroke of genius. He took off his jacket and sat down in his shirtsleeves. It was a bohemian touch of freedom that charms and excites and brings out the young girl that's always inside a respectable woman. She, too, tossed her hat, a two-hundred franc hat, into the corner of the room, stretched out her arms and gave off this heartfelt shout:

"*Ah, oui, que c'est bon de se desembêter!*"[25]

And then, as the Spanish say, *la mar*. The sun, as it took its leave of the earth that day, found them still in Viroflay, still in the little inn, still in the room, and at the table once more over a comforting beefsteak, as events ordered urgently and logically.

Versailles was forgotten. It was a matter of getting back to the station to catch the Paris train. She slowly tied the ribbons of her hat, picked up one of the flowers on the windowsill and placed it in her bosom, took a slow look around the room and the bedchamber so she would remember and retain it, and they left. At the station, as they got into different compartments (because of their arrival in Paris), Chambray, with a squeeze of the hand, hasty and weak now, begged her to tell him her name at least. She whispered "Lucie."

"And that's all I know about her," Chambray concluded, lighting his cigar. "And I also know that she's married, because at the Gare Saint-Lazare, waiting for her, accompanied by a grave lackey from a bourgeois household, was her husband. He's a chocolate-colored *rastacuero* with a thin little beard and an enormous pearl in his tie . . . Poor devil, he was charmed when she gave him a big bouquet of yellow carnations that I'd bought for her in Viroflay . . . A delightful woman. There's nothing like French women!"

What do you have to say about these notable things, my dear Ramalho? I say, summing up, that this world of ours is perfect and in all space there's none that's better organized. Because you will note how at the end of this Sunday in May all three of these excellent creatures, from a simple trip to Versailles, got something positive out of life. Chambray experienced an immense pleasure and an immense vanity, the only two results he expects as solid returns from existence, making the work of existing worthwhile for him. Madame experienced a new or different sensation, which invigorated and unburdened her, allowed her to reenter more calmly the monotony of her home and be of use to those around her with a renewed application. And the Argentine acquired another unexpected and triumphal certainty of how loved he was and how fortunate he had been in his choice. Three fortunate people at the end of that spring day in the country. And if a child is the result of it (the son that the Argentine is eager to have), and if he inherits the strong and glowingly Gallic qualities of Chambray, there will be, in addition to the individual contentment of the three, a definite profit for society. This world, therefore, has been organized in a superior way.

Your faithful friend who faithfully awaits your return from Holland,

Fradique

VII
To Madame de Jouarre
(Transl.)
LISBON, MARCH

My dear Godmother,

It was yesterday, when I arrived in Lisbon at the dead of night from the north and Porto, that returning suddenly to my stunned memory was the oath I had taken on Easter Saturday in Paris, with my hands laid piously on your magnificent edition of Cicero's *Duties*. A foolhardy oath it was, to send you by mail from Portugal every week "descriptions, notes, reflections, and panoramas," as can be read in the subtitle of the *Trip to Switzerland* by your friend the Baron of Fernay, a Commander of the Order of Charles III and a member of the Academy of Toulouse. And I fulfill my oaths (when taken on Cicero's moral code and for the enjoyment of someone who holds sway over my will) with such fidelity, that no sooner did I remember than I opened both eyes wide in order to gather "descriptions, notes, reflections, and panoramas" of this land that is mine and is *a la disposición de usted* . . .[26] We had arrived at a station called Sacavém, and all that my wide-open eyes saw of my country through the foggy windows of the railroad car was a thick darkness, where seen faintly here and there were distant, vague little lights. They were the lights on barges sleeping on the river, and they symbolized in a rather humiliating way those scarce, faint bits of positive truth man is given to discover in the universal mystery of being. So I closed my eyes once more with resignation until a man in a cap with braid, his jacket dripping wet, came to the compartment door and asked for my ticket, calling me *Vossa Excelência*, Your Excellency! In Portugal, my dear Godmother, we are all nobles, we all take part in the State, and we all call each other *Excellency*.

It was Lisbon and it was raining. There were only a few of us on the train, thirty perhaps, simple folk with light suitcases and plain cloth bags, who quickly went through the paternal and sleepy customs inspection and immediately disappeared into the city and the wet March night.

In the gloomy terminal, waiting for the serious baggage, were Smith and I and a tall, thin lady with glasses poised on the tip of her long nose, wrapped up in an old fur coat. It must have been two o'clock in the morning. The filthy asphalt of the floor was freezing our feet.

I don't know how many centuries we waited like that, Smith not moving, the lady and I walking separately and rapidly in order to stay warm along the length of the wooden counter where customs guards, skin dark as olives, were yawning with dignity. Out of a rear door a cart finally came, on which our heap of luggage was wobbling as the cart moved sluggishly along. The lady with the stork beak immediately recognized her tin-plated trunk, the lid of which, falling back, revealed to my observant eyes (at your service, my demanding Godmother!) a soiled dressing gown, a small box of candy, a missal, and two curling irons. The guard plunged his arm under these intimate objects and with a merciful gesture declared that customs was satisfied. The lady hurried off.

Smith and I were left there by ourselves. Smith had already painstakingly gathered my luggage together. But a leather bag was inexplicably missing, and, silently and with the list in his hand, a porter was making a slow search through the bundles, barrels, packages, and old trunks stored in the rear against the stained wall. I watched that worthy man hesitate thoughtfully over a canvas bundle, then over a pine chest. Could either of these have been the leather bag? Finally, dispirited, he declared that among those pieces of luggage there was positively nothing leather, no bag. Smith protested, irritated now. Then the foreman snatched the list from the inept hands of the porter and with his superior intelligence of a chief undertook a search through all the "entries" again, scrutinizing crates, barrels, casks, hat boxes, baskets, cans, and demijohns. In the end he shrugged his shoulders with unspeakable tedium and disappeared inside, in the direction of the darkness of the inner platforms. After a few minutes he returned, scratching his head under his cap, casting his eyes around over the empty floor, expecting the bag to burst forth from the bowels of this desolate globe. Nothing! Impatiently, I undertook myself an anxious search through the building. The customs guard, a cigarette hanging from his lip (bless him!), was also casting a helpful and magisterial eye here and there. Nothing! Suddenly, however, a woman with a red kerchief around her head, who had been loitering about on that crude and early dawn, pointed to the station entrance.

"Is that it there, sir?"

It was! It was my bag, outside by the entrance in the drizzle. I didn't ask how it got to be there all by itself, separated from the luggage to which it was strictly attached by the routing number printed on the list in large figures. And I asked for a carriage. The porter threw his jacket over his head, went out onto the square, and returned immediately, announcing that there were no cabs.

"No cabs! That's a good one! How, then, do passengers get away from here?"

The man shrugged his shoulders. "Sometimes there were, and sometimes there weren't. It all depends . . ." I flashed a five-tostão coin and begged that worthy person to run through the neighborhood in search of any kind of wheeled vehicle, cart or coach, that could bear me away to the comforts of a bowl of soup and a fireplace. The man went off muttering and I, as a disgruntled patriot, turned to the foreman and the customs guard and inveighed against the irregularity of that service. In all the stations of the world, even in Tunis, even in Romelia, when trains arrived there were buses, carts, carriages to carry people and their baggage . . . Why weren't there any in Lisbon? We have such abominable service that it's a dishonor to the nation!

The customs man made a sad gesture, showing full awareness that all services were abominable and that the whole country was nothing but a matter of irreparable disorder. Then, as consolation, he took a full drag on his cigarette. That was how one of those quarter hours that bring on wrinkles to human faces went by.

The porter finally returned, shaking off the rain and announcing that there wasn't a single cab to be had in the whole neighborhood of Santa Apolónia.

"So what am I to do? Am I stuck here?"

The foreman advised me to leave the luggage and that the following morning, with the certainty of a carriage (ordered in writing perhaps), it could be picked up at my convenience. That separation did not coincide with my convenience, however. Well, then, he didn't see any solution unless some late-night lost cab should happen to come that way.

So, like castaways on a desert island in the Pacific, we all huddled by the station entrance waiting for the appearance through the darkness of some rescuing sail—I mean rescuing carriage. A bitter wait, a sterile wait! No light of a lantern, no sound of any wheels cutting the silence of those barren parts.

Fed up, completely fed up, the foreman declared that "it was going on three o'clock" and he wanted to close up the station. What about me? Was I supposed to stay there on the street in the harsh night, tied to a pile of non-transportable luggage? No! In the heart of the worthy foreman there surely must have been more pity. Touched, the man thought of another solution. And it was for us, Smith and me, with the help of a porter, to pick up the baggage and go off to a hotel carrying it on our backs. Actually, that did seem to be the only recourse for our troubles. Smith and I, however (seeing how much backs softened by long and delightful years of civilization abhor the carrying of bundles and how tenacious remains the hope of those to whom fate has persisted in showing a loving face), went out again in silence into the square, plumbing the darkness with ears tilted toward the pavement, listening anxiously that we might hear perhaps, far away, the rolling toward us of the carriage that Providence was sending us. Nothing. Absolutely, desolately nothing in those stingy shadows! . . . My dear Godmother, with all these events, by now the teardrops must be dancing on your compassionate eyelids. I didn't weep, but instead I was ashamed, taken with a great gnawing shame before Smith. What would that Scotsman be thinking of my country—and of me, his master, a part of that disorganized country? There's nothing more fragile than the reputation of nations. One simple cab missing at night and there you have, in the mind of the foreigner, a thorough disbelief in an entire age-old civilization!

But the foreman was steaming. It was three o'clock (three-fifteen even) and he wanted to close up the station. What was there to do? In despair, sighing, we were left with the decision. I grabbed the traveling case and the bundle of blankets, Smith laid onto his respectable shoulders, virgin of any loads, a thick leather suitcase, and the porter was moaning under the huge steel-reinforced trunk. And (leaving two items to be picked up the next day) we started out in a somber single file, waddling over the distance between Santa Apolónia and the Hotel de Braganza. A few steps along, as the traveling case was wearying out my arm, I hoisted it up onto my back . . . And all three of us, heads lowered, backs crushed by the poundage, with an intense sourness ruining our livers, went along slowly in a gloomy single file, advancing into the capital city of this realm! I'd come to Lisbon with the aim of getting some rest and comfort. This was the comfort, this was the rest. There, in that impertinent drizzle, puffing, sweating, stumbling on the ill-placed stones of a dark street, working like a porter! . . .

I don't know how many eternities we spent on that *Via Dolorosa*. I do know that suddenly (as if our guardian angel were holding its reins) a carriage, an honest to goodness carriage, broke out of the darkness of an alleyway. Three avid, desperate shouts brought the team to a halt and the luggage all fell like an avalanche onto the old chaise under the feet of the coachman, who, startled and thinking he was being attacked, raised his whip, cursing angrily. But he calmed down, realizing his stupendous omnipotence, and declared that to the Hotel de Braganza (a distance not much greater than the entire Champs Elysées) he couldn't take me for less than *three mil-réis*. Eighteen francs in coin, silver or gold, for a short run in this democratic and industrial age, after all the hard work of science and revolutions to equalize and get rid of social injustices. Trembling with anger but submissive, like one yielding to the demands of a blunderbuss, I climbed into the cab, after taking leave with great affection of the porter, our faithful comrade on that arduous night.

We finally went off at a desperate gallop. Moments later we were assaulting the sleeping door of the Hotel de Braganza with all manner of violence and seduction, pounding, shouting, punching, kicking, cursing, and wailing. In vain! The golden portal of the Palace of Good Fortune had been no more resistant to the handsome Sir Percival. Finally the coachman threw himself against it, kicking. And with a better understanding of his language, no doubt, the door slowly and sleepily rolled back on its hinges. Thanks be to God, ineffable Father, at last we were under a roof and amidst the carpeting and stucco of progress after such a barbarous experience. All that remained was to pay the pounder. I went over to him with sour sarcasm:

"So it's three mil-réis, then?"

By the light of the vestibule that was hitting my face the man was smiling. What, then, was the reply of that unequalled scoundrel going to be?

"I only said that to say something . . . I didn't recognize you, Senhor Dom Fradique . . . For Senhor Dom Fradique it's whatever you wish."

Incomparable humiliation! I immediately felt some kind of dull mellowing that was softening my heart. It was the good fellowship, the lax weakness that binds us Portuguese together, fills us up with guilty indulgence toward one another, and irrevocably destroys all order and discipline among us. Yes, my dear Godmother . . . That bandit knew Senhor Dom Fradique. He had a rascally and accommodating smile. We were both Portuguese. I gave the bandit a pound!

And here you have for your education the true way in which, in this last quarter of the nineteenth century, one enters Portugal's great city.

The one who always finds it painful to be away from you,

Fradique

VIII

To Mr. E. Mollinet

Editor of the *Review of Biography and History*

PARIS, SEPTEMBER

My dear Mr. Mollinet,

On my return from Fontainebleau yesterday evening I found on my night table the letter in which you, my learned friend, in the name and interests of the *Review of Biography and History*, ask me who this countryman of mine Pacheco (José Joaquim Alves Pacheco) is, he whose death is being so widely and sadly lamented in the newspapers of Portugal. And you, my friend, would also like to know what works, what attainments, what books, what ideas, or what contribution to Portuguese civilization the said Pacheco has left, given that such loud and reverent weeping has followed him to his grave.

I only knew Pacheco casually. I possess a mental summary of sorts of his figure and his life. Pacheco didn't leave his country any work, attainment, book, or idea. Pacheco was superior and illustrious among us for the simple reason that *he had immense talent.* Yet, my dear Mr. Mollinet, that talent, which two generations acclaimed so wondrously, never gave us any positive, expressive, or visible manifestation of its strength. Pacheco's immense talent always remained silent, withdrawn in Pacheco's depths. His life was a constant passage through eminent social positions: deputy, director-general, minister, director of banks, member of the State Council, peer, prime minister—Pacheco was everything, had everything in this country, which watched from a distance and at his feet, amazed at his talent. But never in these situations, either for his own benefit or for the urgency of the state, did Pacheco find any need to release, assert, or let operate outside of himself the immense talent that he kept muffled inside. When friends, political parties, newspapers, departments, collective bodies, and the whole compact mass of the nation whispering "Such immense talent!" about Pacheco invited him to expand his domain and his fortune, Pacheco would smile, lower his grave eyes behind his gold-rimmed glasses, and continue along, always upward, always higher through institutions, with his immense talent closed up in his skull as in a miser's strongbox. And that reserve, that smile, that flash of his eyeglasses was enough for the country, which felt and savored in all of it the resplendent evidence of Pacheco's talent.

That talent had its birth in Coimbra, in classes in Natural Law on one morning when Pacheco, rejecting the lecture notes, stated that "the nineteenth century was a century of progress and enlightenment." The class thereupon began to sense and affirm in cafés in the market that there was a lot of talent in Pacheco. And this admiration of the class, growing every day, spreading, like all religious movements, from the impressionable masses to the reasoning classes, from students to professors, easily brought Pacheco a *prize* at the end of the year. The fame of that talent then spread throughout the whole academic world, which, seeing Pacheco always meditative, wearing glasses now, austere in his walk, with thick briefs under his arm, perceived a great spirit there, one concentrated and taut, with complete inner strength. This academic generation, as it scattered about, brought to the most primitive back-country villages in the land word of Pacheco's immense talent. And now in the shadowy pharmacies of Trás-os-Montes, in the garrulous barbershops of the Algarve, people were saying with respect and with hope: "It seems there's a young fellow just graduated who's got a lot of talent, Pacheco!"

Pacheco was ripe for national performance. He entered its bosom, brought in by a government (I can't remember which one) that had managed, through disbursements and wiles, to take control of Pacheco's precious talent. Then, on that starry December night in Lisbon when he went to have tea and toast at Martinho's, it was whispered about among the tables, with curiosity, "That's Pacheco, a young chap with loads of talent!" And since the Parliament went into session, all the eyes of the government as well as those of the opposition began to turn insistently, almost anxiously, on Pacheco, who, sitting on the edge of his bench, maintained his look of a thoughtful recluse, his arms folded over a velvet vest, his head tilted to the side as if under the weight of its inner riches, and his eyeglasses sparkling . . .

Finally, one afternoon, during arguments about the reply to the Crown speech, Pacheco made a movement as if to interrupt a cross-eyed priest who was delivering a harangue about "freedom." The prelate immediately halted out of deference, the recording clerks voraciously cocked their ears, and the whole Chamber ceased its unencumbered whispering so that in a properly majestic silence, for the first time, Pacheco's immense talent might come forth. Pacheco, however, was not so prodigal with his treasures right off. Standing with his finger raised in a gesture that was very much his, Pacheco stated in a tone betraying the assurance of his innermost thought and wisdom that "freedom must always coexist with authority!" Not much, of course, but the chamber understood quite well that under that brief summary lay a world, a whole formidable world of solid ideas. It was months before he spoke again, but his talent inspired all the more respect the more invisible and inaccessible it was kept inside, in the rich and populated depth of his being. The only recourse left, then, to the devotees of that immense talent (whom it already possessed in uncountable numbers) was to contemplate Pacheco's brow, the way one gazes at heaven with the certainty that God is up there behind it, disposing. Pacheco's brow offered a beveled surface, broad and lustrous. And many times, concerning him, counselors and director-generals would babble with amazement, "All you have to do is just look at that head!"

Pacheco immediately became part of the main parliamentary committees. He never deigned, however, to outline any project, disdainful of specializations. Only now and then would he silently jot down some slow note. And when he emerged from his concentration and lifted up his finger it was to deliver himself of some general idea about order, progress, development, or the economy. There you had the obvious aspect of an immense talent, which (as his friends would whisper with a delicate wink) "was waiting up there, hovering." Besides, Pacheco himself was teaching (sketching out with his fat hand the higher flight of a wing up over the tree tops) the lesson that "a true talent should only know things *by their branches.*"

This immense talent couldn't help but be of aid to Crown councils. In a ministerial shuffling (brought on by embezzlement) Pacheco became a minister, and there was an immediate perception of what a strong consolidation of power would be forthcoming from Pacheco's immense talent. In his ministry (which was that of the Navy), during the long months of his management, Pacheco did "absolutely nothing," as three or four embittered and narrowly factual spirits insinuated. But, for the first time with this regime, the nation stopped suffering anxieties and doubts concerning our colonial empire. Why? Because it felt that the supreme interests of that empire had finally been entrusted to a talent that was immense: the immense talent of Pacheco.

In the government seats, Pacheco very rarely rose up out of his complete and fruitful silence. Sometimes, however, when the opposition became clamorous, Pacheco would reach out his arm and slowly jot down a note in pencil; that note, set down with wisdom and a most mature thought, would be enough to upset the opposition and make it recoil. The fact is, Pacheco's immense talent ended up inspiring a disciplinary terror in the chambers, on committees, and in centers of activity. Woe to anyone on whom that immense talent were to be unleashed with wrath! Certain for him was irredeemable humiliation. This was painfully felt by the pedagogist who one day was bold enough to accuse the Honorable Minister of the Kingdom (Pacheco was directing internal affairs then) of neglecting education in the country. No accusation could have been more deeply sensitive for that immense spirit who, in his lapidary and lush phrase, had taught that "a people without secondary schooling is an incomplete people." Holding up his finger (always his signature gesture), Pacheco crushed the foolhardy man with this tremendous item: "To the illustrious deputy who censures me I can only say that, in matters of public education, while Your Excellency goes about braying among those benches, here in this chair I shed light!" I was in the gallery during that splendid moment and I cannot remember ever having heard in a human gathering such a passionate and fervid wave of applause. I think it was a few days later that Pacheco received the Grand Cross of the Order of Sant'Iago.

Pacheco's immense talent was gradually becoming a national credo. Seeing how much unwavering support that immense talent was giving to the institutions that it served, all hungered after him. Pacheco began to be the universal board member of companies and banks. Sought after by the Crown, he joined the Council of State. His party avidly demanded that he be made its leader and the other parties, more and more and with submissive reverence, sought the help of his immense talent. The nation was slowly becoming concentrated in Pacheco.

As he thus grew older and his influence and dignity increased, the admiration for his immense talent began to take on, across the nation, certain forms of expression fitting only for religion and love. When he was prime minister, there were devotees who would place their hands over their hearts piously, lifting up their eyes to heaven, and whisper devoutly, "Ah, such talent!" And there were those in love who would kiss the tips of their fingers and babble languidly, "Ah, what talent . . ." And also, why hide it? There were others for whom that immense talent was bitterly irritating, as an excessive and disproportionate privilege. I heard these roar with fury and stamp their feet, saying, "Damn it, that's having too much talent!" Pacheco, meanwhile, had nothing more to say. He would simply smile. His brow was getting broader and broader.

I won't go over his incomparable career. All you have to do, my dear Mr. Mollinet, is thumb through our annals. In all institutions, reforms, foundations, works you will find Pacheco's stamp. All Portugal, morally and socially, is replete with Pacheco. He was everything, he had everything. His talent was immense, of course! Immense too, however, was recognition by his country. Pacheco and Portugal, after all, had an irreplaceable need for each other and they were a perfect fit. Without Portugal, Pacheco would not have been what he was among men and, without Pacheco, Portugal would not have been what it is among nations.

His old age had an august character to it. He had lost his hair completely. He was all forehead. And he was revealing his immense talent more than ever, even in the tiniest of things. I remember quite well the night (he was prime minister then) when, in the salon of the Countess of Arrodes, someone had eagerly wanted to know what His Excellency thought of Cánovas del Castillo. Silently, magisterially, His Excellency, only smiling, made a slight horizontal slice through the air with his grave hand. And all about there were slow and amazed whispers of admiration. In that gesture there were so many subtle and deeply thought out things! I, for my part, after much digging about, interpreted it in this way, "Mediocre and middling is Señor Cánovas!" Because, remember, my dear Mr. Mollinet, that that talent, while being so vast, was at the same time so subtle.

He croaked—I mean His Excellency died—almost suddenly, without any suffering, at the beginning of this harsh winter. He was just about to be made the Marquis of Pacheco. The whole nation wept with infinite grief. He lies in the Alto de São João cemetery in a mausoleum in front of which, at the suggestion of Counselor Acácio (in a letter to the *Diário de Notícias*), the figure of *Portugal Mourning Her Genius* has been erected.

Some months after Pacheco's death, I ran into his widow in Sintra, at the home of Dr. Videira. She is a woman (my friends assure me) of excellent intelligence and kindness. Fulfilling the duties of a Portuguese, I lamented before that illustrious and affable lady the irreparable loss for her and for the nation. But when, touched with emotion, I alluded to Pacheco's immense talent, Pacheco's widow, with brusque astonishment, raised the eyes she had kept lowered, and a fleeting, sad, almost pitying smile tucked up the corners of her pale mouth . . . The eternal mismatches of human destinies! That average woman had never understood that immense talent!

I remain, my dear Mr. Mollinet, your dedicated

Fradique

IX

To Clara . . .

(Transl.)

PARIS, JUNE

My adored friend,

No, it wasn't at the watercolor exhibition in March that I had my first meeting with you, by command of the Fates. It was during the winter, my adored
friend, at the Tressans' ball. It was there that I saw you chatting with Madame
de Jouarre in front of a console whose lights, among the bunches of orchids,
were placing over your hair that golden halo which so rightly belongs to you as
"Queen of Grace among Women." I still remember, quite religiously, your weary
smile, your black gown with golden yellow details, and the antique fan folded
in your lap. I passed by, but then everything around me seemed irreparably irk-
some and ugly, and I turned to admire your beauty once more and silently *ponder* it as it went on capturing me with its patently understandable splendor,
along with something it had that was delicate, spiritual, sorrowful, and tender
shining through and coming from your soul. And so intensely had I been absorbed in that contemplation that I carried your image with me, learned by
heart in its entirety, without forgetting a hair on your head or a fold in the silk
that covered you, and I ran off to closet myself with it, all excited, like an artist
who in some dark storeroom, in the midst of dust and dirt, has discovered a
sublime work by a perfect master.

So why not confess it? That image was for me at first only a painting hanging
in the depths of my soul, one which I kept looking at, but only to praise, with
growing surprise, its various charms of line and color. It was only a rare canvas,
placed in a sanctuary, motionless and mute in its brilliance, with no other influence over me than the kind exercised by a very beautiful form that captivates
a very refined taste. My being remained free, attent on the curiosities that up
till then had seduced it, open to the sentiments that up till then had attracted
it. And only when I felt weariness with imperfect things or a new desire for a
purer occupation, I would return to the image that I kept inside me, like a Fra
Angelico in his cloister, laying down his brushes at the end of the day and kneeling before the Madonna, imploring her for repose and superior inspiration.

Gradually, however, everything that wasn't that contemplation was losing
value and charm for me. Every day I began to live more withdrawn into the
depths of my soul, lost in admiration for the image that shined there, until only
that occupation seemed worthy of life to me. In all the world I recognized only

one inconstant appearance, and I was like a monk in his cell, alien to things more real, kneeling and rigid in his dream, which for him is the only reality.

But it was not, my adored friend, a pale and passive ecstasy before your image. No! Rather it was an anxious and strong study of it, as I tried to know the Essence through the Form and (since Beauty is the splendor of Truth) deduce from the perfections of your Body the superiorities of your Soul. And that was how I slowly discovered the secret of your nature. Your clear forehead that your hair reveals, so clear and smooth, told me immediately of the rectitude of your thought. Your smile, of such intellectual nobility, easily revealed to me your disdain for worldly and ephemeral things, your tireless aspiration for a life of truth and beauty. Every one of your graceful movements betrayed to me the refinement of your taste, and in your eyes I could distinguish what was so adorably mingled in them, the light of reason together with the warmth of your heart, a light that warms better, a warmth that lights better . . . The certainty of so many perfections would already be enough to bend the most rebellious knees in a perpetual adoration. But it so happened that, as I gradually understood you and your essence was showing itself to me, visible like that and almost tangible, an influence was descending over me, a strange influence, different from all human influences and one which was dominating me with overreaching omnipotence. How can I put it? A monk locked in my cell, I began to aspire to sainthood in order to harmonize myself with and make myself worthy of the saint to whom I had become devoted. Then I put myself through a strict examination of conscience. I investigated, uneasily, whether or not my thinking was deserving of the purity of your thinking, whether in my taste there might not be some disharmony that could wound the discipline of your taste, whether my idea of life was as high and as serious as the one I sensed in the spirituality of your gaze and your smile, and whether my heart had not diminished and weakened too much to be able to beat with the same parallel vigor as yours. And I have in me now a gasping effort to climb up to perfection identical to the one I so submissively adore in you.

So, my beloved friend, without knowing it you became my instructor. And so dependent did I then become on that schooling that I can no longer conceive of the movements of my being except as governed by it and ennobled by it. I know perfectly well that everything of any value that rises up in me today, an idea or a feeling, is the work of that instruction which your soul is giving mine from afar just by being and being understood. If your influence were to abandon me today—I should have said, rather, like an ascetic, your Grace—all of me would tumble into an unremitting inferiority. See, then, how necessary and precious you have become for me . . . And consider how, in order to exercise that saving supremacy, your hands had no need to lay themselves on mine; it was enough for me to catch sight of you at a party, resplendent in the distance. Just the way a wild shrub can bloom alongside a sinkhole, because there above in the distant skies a great sun that doesn't see it or know it nevertheless magnanimously makes it grow, burst into bloom, and give off its quick aroma . . . For that reason my love attains the indescribable and nameless feeling that the plant, if it had feeling, would have had for the light.

So consider still that, needing you like that light, I beg nothing of you, I implore no favor from one who can do so much and is for me the mistress of all good things. All I wish for is that you let me live under the influence that emanates from the simple glow of your perfections and so easily and so sweetly works toward my betterment. All I ask for is that charitable permission. See, then, how I keep myself distant and vague in the sculpted humility of an adoration that is even fearful that its whispering, the whispers of a prayer, will brush the garment of the holy image . . .

But if by any chance you, my beloved friend, certain of my renunciation of any earthly recompense, would allow me to unfold before you the agitated secret of my breast on some solitary day, you would really be performing an act of ineffable mercy, just as in times gone by the Virgin Mary would fortify her worshippers, hermits and saints, by descending in a cloud and awarding them a fleeting smile or letting fall into their outstretched hands a rose from Paradise. Therefore, tomorrow I am going to spend the afternoon with Madame de Jouarre. There will be no sanctity of a cell or a hermitage there, but there will be something like its isolation, and if you, my beloved friend, were to appear in full splendor and I were to receive from you, I won't say a rose, but a smile, then I would be radiantly certain that this love of mine or this indescribable and nameless feeling that goes beyond love would find before your eyes pity and permission to hope.

Fradique

X

To Madame de Jouarre
(Transl.)

LISBON, JUNE

My excellent Godmother,

Behold what your admirable godson has "seen and done" since May in the most lovely Lisbon, *Ulyssipo pulcherrima*! I have discovered a countryman of mine from the Islands and a relative, who has been living for three years constructing a system of philosophy on the third floor of a boarding house on the Travessa da Palha. A free spirit, enterprising and clever, a paladin of general ideas, my relative, Procópio by name, feeling that a woman is not worth the torment she spreads about her and that 800 mil-réis from an olive grove is more than sufficient for a man of the spirit, has devoted his life to logic and is only interested in and suffers for the truth. He is a merry philosopher, he converses without bellowing, he has some excellent muscatel brandy, and it is with pleasure that two or three times a week I climb up to his metaphysics workshop to find out whether, led by the sweet soul of Maine de Biran, his guide on trips to the Infinite, he has caught a glimpse at last, disguised behind its last remaining veils, of the Cause of Causes. On these prayerful visits I have gradually come to know some of the boarders who, on that third floor of the Travessa da Palha, are enjoying a good city life for twelve tostões a day, excepting wine and clean clothes. Almost all the professions in which the middle class in Portugal occupies itself are faithfully represented here, so therefore I can study without any effort, as in an index, the ideas and sentiments that make up in this year of Our Lord the moral base of the nation.

This boarding house has its delights. My cousin Procópio's room has a new mat, a philosophical and virginal iron bed, fancy muslins on the windows, birds and tiny roses on the walls, and it undergoes a strict cleaning by one of those maidservants that only Portugal produces, a pretty girl from Trás-os-Montes who, dragging her slippers along with the grave indolence of a Latin nymph, sweeps, dusts, and tidies up the whole floor. She serves nine lunches, nine dinners, and nine teas; she washes the dishes; she sews on the buttons that Portuguese men are always losing from their long johns and trousers; she starches Madam's skirts; she prays her village rosary; and, apart from all this, she still has time to be in love with a neighborhood barber who is all set to marry her when he gets a job at the customhouse. (And all this on the pay of three mil-réis.) At lunch there are two courses, healthful and plentiful, of eggs and beef. The wine comes straight from the farm, a light and precocious little wine made from the venerable recipes found in the Georgics, similar no doubt to the wine from Raetia—*quo te carmine dicam, Rethica?*[27] The toast, made over the strong fire, is incomparable. And the four pictures that adorn the parlor, a portrait of Fontes (a statesman, dead now, held in great veneration by the Portuguese), Pius IX, smiling and giving his blessing, a view of the fields of Colares, and two damsels kissing a turtledove, inspire the so-needed wholesome ideas of social order, faith, rustic peace, and innocence.

The landlady, Dona Paulina Soriana, is a Madame of some forty Octobers, chubby and well kept, with a rather thick neck, and her whole person is whiter than the white housecoat she wears over a purple silk skirt. She appears to be an excellent lady, patient and maternal, with good judgment and thrifty. Without exactly being a widow, she has a son, already getting fat as well, who bites his nails and is in secondary school. His name is Joaquim, lovingly nicknamed Quinzinho. This spring he suffered from some kind of severe illness that forced endless milky cordials and hip baths on him, and Dona Paulina destines him for the bureaucracy, which she considers, and quite rightly so, as the most secure and the easiest of careers.

"The best thing for a young fellow (the appreciable lady affirmed a few days ago after lunch, crossing her legs) is to have patrons and get a job. Then he'll be all set, not too much work and the little old paycheck right there at the end of the month."

But Dona Paulina is not anxious about Quinzinho's career. Through the influence (which is all-powerful in these realms) of a sure friend, Counselor Vaz Neto, at the Ministry of Public Works or at Justice there already is a position of Secretary reserved, marked out, and waiting for Quinzinho. And even though Quinzinho failed his last exams, Counselor Vaz Neto already reminded him that, as he was lax and showed very little interest in letters, it was best not to pursue his studies any further and to go into the Department right away . . .

"But even so (the good lady added when she honored me with these confidences) I still would like Quinzinho to finish his schooling. It wouldn't be because of necessity or because of the job, as you can see, it would be for the satisfaction."

So Quinzinho has his prosperity all nicely guaranteed. As for the rest, I imagine that Dona Paulina has put aside a prudent bit of money. In the house, well taken care of, there are now seven boarders, all of them faithful, solid, and spending, with extras, from forty-five to fifty mil-réis a month. The oldest and the most respected (and precisely the one I know already) is Pinho: Pinho the

Brazilian, Comendador Pinho. It is he who announces the time for breakfast every morning (the hall clock has been out of order since Christmas), coming out of his room punctually at ten o'clock with his bottle of Vidago water, on his way to occupy at the already set table his chair, a special wicker chair with an air cushion. No one knows the age of this Pinho, about his family, the part of the countryside where he was born, the work he did in Brazil, or the origins of his rank. He arrived one winter afternoon on a Royal Mail packet, spent five days in quarantine, disembarked with two trunks, the wicker chair, and fifty-six cans of guava marmalade, took his room in this boarding house with a window on the Travessa, and here he grows fat peacefully and pleasantly with the six percent from his investments. He's a paunchy, stubby fellow, with a graying beard and dark skin, all in tones of brick and coffee, always dressed in black cashmere, with a pair of gold-trimmed pince-nez spectacles hanging from a silk thread, which on the street, at every corner, he will disentangle from his gold watch chain in order to read, slowly and with interest, the theater posters. His life has one of those prudent regularities that so admirably come together to create order in nations. After breakfast he puts on his low-cut boots, shines his silk hat, and goes off very slowly to the Rua dos Capelistas, to the ground-floor office of the broker Godinho, where he spends two hours perched on a stool next to the counter, his hairy hands resting on the handle of his umbrella. Afterwards he tucks the umbrella under his arm and goes along the Rua do Ouro, with a delightful laziness, stopping to contemplate some lady in flaring silks or some victoria with liveried footmen, then continuing his steps to Sousa the tobacconist in the Rossio, where he has a glass of Caneças water and there takes his ease until the afternoon cools off. Then he continues on to the Avenida, enjoying the pure air and the splendor of the city as he sits on a bench, or he may take a turn about the Rossio under the trees, his face held high and glowing with well-being. At six o'clock he returns, takes off and folds his frock coat, puts on his slippers of Morocco leather and a comfortable cotton jacket, and dines, always having a second helping of soup. After coffee he takes a "hygienic" stroll through the Baixa, with thoughtful but pleasant pauses at the windows of sweet shops and fashion stores, and on certain days he goes up to the Chiado, turns the corner of the Rua Nova da Trindade, and bargains, calmly but firmly, for a ticket to the Ginásio. Every Friday he enters his bank, which is the London Brazilian. On Sundays at dusk he discreetly visits a stout, clean mistress who lives on the Rua da Madalena. Every six months he collects the interest on his investments.

In this way his entire existence is a methodical rest. Nothing upsets him, nothing excites him. The universe for Comendador Pinho consists of two entities only: himself, Pinho, and the State, which provides him with his six percent. The whole universe, therefore, is in perfect shape, and life is perfect just as long as Pinho, thanks to Vidago water, maintains a good appetite and good health, and the State continues faithfully to pay his dividends. As for the rest, he needs very little to satisfy that portion of body and soul of which he is apparently composed. The necessity that all living creatures (even oysters, as naturalists will attest) have to communicate with their fellows by means of gestures and sounds is not very demanding in Pinho. Around the middle of April, he will smile and say, unfolding his napkin, "We have summer with us." Everyone agrees and Pinho is pleased. Around the middle of October he will stroke his beard and softly say, "We have winter with us." If another boarder disagrees, Pinho will say nothing, because he's afraid of arguments. And this chaste exchange of ideas is enough for him. At table, as long as he is served a succulent soup in a deep dish, of which he may have two helpings, he is consoled and prepared to give thanks to God. The *Diário de Pernambuco*, the *Diário de Notícias*, some comedy at the Ginásio or a magic show are more than enough to satisfy those other needs for intelligence and imagination that Humboldt found even among the Botocudos. In his sentimental activities Pinho only modestly wants (as he revealed to my cousin one day) "not to come down with any illness." And as for the ultimate destiny of his soul, Pinho (as he assured me) "only desired that after death they wouldn't bury me alive." Even about such an important matter for a comendador as his tomb, Pinho requires very little: just a smooth and decent slab with his name and a simple "Pray for him."

We would be mistaken, however, my dear Godmother, in supposing that Pinho is alien to everything human. No! I am sure that Pinho loves and respects humanity. It's just that humanity for him has become excessively restricted over the course of his life. Men, serious men, those who truly merit that noble name and are worthy of being shown reverence and affection, and for whom one can risk a not too wearying step, for Pinho consist only of government bondholders. So my cousin Procópio, with a malice quite unexpected in a spiritualist, told him in confidence a while back that I was owner of a lot of stock, many shares, a lot of investments . . . Well, on my next visit to the boarding house after that revelation, Pinho, blushing slightly, almost emotional, offered me a small box of guava marmalade wrapped in a napkin. A touching act that explains that soul. Pinho is no egoist, no Diogenes in a black dress coat drily withdrawn into the barrel of his uselessness. No. There is in him the complete human wish to love his fellow man and to benefit him. Except that, who for Pinho are his real "fel-

low creatures"? The bondholders of the State. And what does that act of beneficence consist of for Pinho? The transfer to others of what is of no use to himself.
Since Pinho doesn't care much for guava, and as soon as he learned I was the
owner of stocks, his fellow creature, a capitalist just like himself, he didn't hesitate, didn't retreat from his human duty and immediately put into practice his
act of beneficence. There he came, blushing and happy, bearing his sweet offering in a napkin.

Is Comendador Pinho a useless citizen? No, certainly not! For the mainte-
nance of stability and solidity in the the social order of the nation there is no
citizen better suited than this Pinho, with his placid habits, his easy assent to
all features of public affairs, his bank account checked on Fridays, his pleasures
reaped with hygienic discretion, his reticence, his inertia. No idea or act will
ever emerge from a Pinho, no affirmation or denial, that could disturb the peace
of the State. Therefore, fat and quiet, glued onto the social organism, not taking
part in its movement but not going against it either, Pinho presents all the characteristics of a sebaceous excrescence. Socially, Pinho is a cyst. Now, there's nothing more inoffensive than a cyst, and in our times, when the State is so full of
morbid elements that live off it like parasites, suck its blood, infect it, and over-
excite it, this inoffensiveness of Pinho's can even (as interests of order are concerned) be considered a meritorious quality. Therefore, as rumor has it, the State
is going to make him a baron. And baron of a title that honors both the State
and Pinho, because there is in it simultaneously a gracious and discreet homage
to both family and religion. Pinho's father's name was Francisco, Francisco José
Pinho. And our friend is going to be made the Baron of São Francisco.

Farewell, my beloved Godmother. We are entering our eighteenth day of
rain! Ever since the beginning of June and the roses, in this country of sun in
the blue shining on the dark earth of olive groves and laurels, beloved of Phoe-
bus, it has been raining, raining in streams of pouring water, right, continuous,
unperturbed, without a breath of wind to make them waver or a ray of light to
make them sparkle, forming, from cloud to street, a smooth texture of damp
and melancholy, where one's soul struggles and is transfixed like a butterfly
caught in a spider's web. We are right in the middle of Verse 17, Chapter 7, of
Genesis. In case these waters from heaven do not cease, I shall conclude that
Jehovah's intentions for this sinful country are diluvian, and judging myself no
less worthy of grace and divine alliance than Noah, I am going to buy some
wood and pitch and make an ark according to the good Hebraic or Assyrian
models. If, perchance, a while from now a white dove comes to beat its wings
against your windowpane, it will be me having made port in Le Havre in my

ark, bearing with me among other animals Pinho and Dona Paulina, so that later on, the waters having receded, Portugal may be repopulated beneficially and the State will always have Pinhos from whom it can ask for a loan of money and chubby Quinzinhos on whom it can spend the money it has requested from Pinho.

Your loving Godson,

Fradique

XI
To Mr. Bertrand B.
(Engineer in Palestine)
PARIS, APRIL

My dear Bertrand,

Quite ironically, today, this Easter Sunday on which the contented heavens have dressed themselves in Easter finery with a blue and gold chasuble and the new lilacs are perfuming my garden to sanctify it, your horrendous letter arrives, telling me that you have completed laying down the tracks for the Jaffa-Jerusalem railway! And you are triumphant! Surely, by the Damascus Gate, with your heavy boots buried in the sands of Jehoshaphat, your umbrella leaning against a prophet's tombstone, your pencil still wandering across the paper, you are smiling expansively and, through your dark glasses, you are contemplating the "line" marked by little flags where soon, smoking and creaking, there will roll from the former Joppa to the former Zion the black train of your dark work. All around the contractors are wiping away the thick sweat of their labors and uncorking bottles of festive beer. And behind you Progress stands stiffly against Herod's walls, all hinged and bolted, and is celebrating too as it rubs its stiff cast-iron hands with a harsh sound.

How well I sense and how well I understand your infamous railroad, oh favorite and fatal son of the School of Bridges and Highways! Nor did I need that plan with which you dazzle me, all with red lines looking like the cuts of a vile knife on noble flesh. It is in Jaffa, the most ancient Joppa, already heroic and holy before the Flood, that your first station, with its platforms and coal bunkers, its scales and signals, and its station master in his braided cap, is rising up in the midst of those orange groves extolled in the Gospels, where Saint

Peter, running to the cries of the women, raised Dorcas, the good weaver, and helped her come out of her tomb. From there the locomotive, with its chintz-lined first-class coaches, will roll impudently over the plain of Sharon, which was so dear to Heaven that even under the brutish tread of the Philistine hordes its anemones and roses would never wither. It will cut through Beth Dagon and mingle the dust of its coal from Cardiff with the age-old dust of the Temple of Baal, which Samson, mute and driven with sadness, brought down with a movement of his shoulders. It will pass above Lydda and with its shrieks terrify the great Saint George who, still in armor, a feathered helmet on his head and an iron glove on his sword, sleeps his earthly rest there. It will take on water through a leather hose from the holy well where the Virgin, during the flight to Egypt, rested under the fig trees and nursed the Christ Child. It will stop in Ramla, which is the old Arimathea ("Arimathea, fifteen minutes!"), village of sweet gardens and of the sweet man who buried the Lord. Through smoke-filled tunnels it will pierce the hills of Judah where the Prophets wept. It will break through the ruins of what had been the citadel and then the tomb of the Maccabees. On an iron bridge it will leap over the gorge where David, in his wanderings, chose stones for his monster-downing sling. It will snake and arch its way through the melancholy valley where Jeremiah lived. It will then befoul Emmaeus, pierce through the Cedron, and finally come to a halt, sweaty, greasy, and filthy with soot, in the valley of Hinnom at the terminal in Jerusalem.

So, my dear Bertrand, I, who am not someone from Bridges and Highways nor a stockholder in the Palestine Railroad Company, only a pilgrim with nostalgia for those beloved places, feel that your work of civilization is a work of profanation. I know quite well, engineer, that Saint Peter resurrecting old Dorcas, the miraculous blooming of the roses of Sharon, the Christ Child drinking during the flight to Egypt under the shade of the trees that the angels went along planting ahead are fables . . . But they are fables that for two thousand years have given enchantment, hope, consoling shelter, and the strength for living to a third of humanity. The places where those stories took place, very simple and very human to be sure, which later on, because of the need the soul has for the divine, have been transformed into that so beautiful Christian mythology, are thereby venerable. In them lived, fought, taught, and suffered, from Jacob to Saint Paul, all the exceptional beings that inhabit Heaven today. Jehovah only showed himself, with terrifying splendor, in those mountains during the time when he visited among men, and Jesus came down into those thoughtful valleys to renew the world. Palestine has always been the preferred residence of the Divinity, so nothing material should disturb its spiritual privacy. And it is painful for the smoke of progress to dirty an air that still preserves the perfume of the passage of the angels and that its iron rails should turn over the soil where the divine footprints have still not faded away.

You smile and accuse the old Palestine of being an incorrigible fount of illusion. But illusion, friend Bertrand, is just as useful as certainty; and for the formation of a total spirit, in order for it to be complete, there must be an entry for fairy tales as well as for the problems of Euclid. Destroying the religious and poetic influence of the Holy Land, just as much for simple hearts as for cultivated intelligence, is a backward step for civilization, the true one at which you do not labor and which has as its main effort the perfecting of the soul rather than strengthening of the body, and even on the side of utility considers a sentiment more useful than a machine. So that locomotives maneuvering through Judaea and Galilee, with their materiality of coal and iron, their inevitable development of hotels, buses, billiards parlors, and gas lights, will inevitably destroy the emotional power of the Land of Miracles because they will modernize it, industrialize it, and banalize it . . .

Where did that spiritual power and influence of Palestine come from? From its having been preserved immutably *biblical* and *evangelical* for over four thousand years . . . Changes did come over Israel, of course. The Turkish administration has been less splendid than the Roman; of the orchards and gardens that encircled Jerusalem only rocks and weeds remain; the cities are tumbledown and have lost their heroism of citadels; wine is rare, learning has been snuffed out, and I have no doubt that here and there in Zion, on some roof terrace of a Levantine merchant someone in the moonlight is whistling the waltz from *Madame Angot.*

But intimate life, in its rural, urban, or nomadic form, with its manners, customs, ceremonies, dress, utensils, everything, remains as it was in the time of Abraham and the time of Jesus. To enter Palestine is to penetrate a living Bible. The goatskin tents pitched in the shade of the sycamore trees, the shepherd leaning on his long crook and followed by his flock, the women in yellow or white veils singing on their way to the fountain with their pitchers on their shoulders, the mountain man shooting at eagles with his sling, the old men sitting in the cool of the evening by the gates of walled villages, the bright terraces filled with doves, the scribe who passes with his inkwell hanging from his belt, the servant girls grinding seeds, the man with long Nazarene hair who greets us with the word "peace" and who speaks in parables, the landlady who takes us in and throws a carpet under our feet as we pass through the doorway to her dwelling, and also the bridal processions and their slow dances to the beat of tambourines, and the professional mourners around the whitened sepulchers—all of it transports the pilgrim to the old Judaea of Scripture and in such a present and real way that we keep wondering if that thin, dark woman with large golden earrings and smelling of sandal who leads a lamb tied to the edge of her cloak might still be Rachel, or if among the men sitting farther off in the shade of a fig tree and a vine the one with a short, curly beard raising his arm might be Jesus, teaching.

That feeling, precious for the believer, is precious for the intellectual, too, because it places him in open communion with one of the most wonderful moments of human history. Of course, it would be equally interesting (more interesting, perhaps) if one could gather the same emotion in Greece and that we could still find there, in its dress, its customs, its sociability, the great Athens of Pericles. Unfortunately, that incomparable Athens lies dead, buried forever, ground into dust under the Roman Athens, the Byzantine Athens, the barbarian Athens, the Muslim Athens, and the constitutional and sordid Athens. Everywhere that old stage of history has been torn up and lies in ruins. The hills themselves, it would seem, have lost their classic configuration, and no one can find in Latium the river and cool valley that Virgil inhabited and of which he sang in such a Virgilian way. Only one place on earth has still kept the look and customs which the men who gave the world one of its highest transformations have seen and partaken of, and that place is a piece of Judaea, Samaria, and Galilee. If it is vulgarly modernized, brought down to the level of prototype desired by this century, the district of Liverpool, say, or the department of Marseilles, and if in that way the educational opportunity of seeing a grand image of the past is lost forever, what a profanation, what a brutish and barbarous devastation it will be! And with the loss of that surviving form of ancient civilizations, the treasure of our inspiration and learning will be irrevocably diminished.

No one certainly appreciates and venerates a railroad more than I, my dear Bertrand, and it would be most painful for me to travel from Paris to Bordeaux the way Jesus came up out of the valley of Jericho to Jerusalem, astride a donkey. The most useful things, however, are intrusive and even scandalous when they vulgarly invade places that are not suited to them. There is nothing more necessary in life than a restaurant and yet no one, no matter how disbelieving or irreverent he might be, would ever think of installing a restaurant, with its tables and clatter of dishes and smell of cooking, in the nave of Notre Dame or the old cathedral of Coimbra. A railroad is a praiseworthy piece of work between Paris and Bordeaux. Between Jericho and Jerusalem, a light mare that rents for two drachmas is quite sufficient, as is the canvas pitched at dusk among the palm trees by a pond of fresh water, where one can sleep so divinely under the radiant peace of the stars of Syria.

And it is that tent, precisely, and the grave camel who carries the baggage, and the brilliant escort of Bedouins, and the portions of desert over which one gallops with his soul full of freedom, and Solomon's lily picked from the crevices of a sacred ruin, and the cool halts by biblical wells, and the recollection of the past at night around the campfire that make up the enchantment of the journey and attract the man of good taste who loves the delicate emotions of nature, history, and art. When traveling from Jerusalem to Galilee is done aboard a screechy, dust-laden railway car, perhaps no one will undertake the magnificent pilgrimage, except for a sharp commercial traveler on his way to sell chintzes from Manchester or red cloth from Sedan in the bazaars. Your dark train will roll along empty. What a pure joy that would be for all understanding and cultivated people, as long as they're not stockholders in the Palestine Railroad Company!

But you may rest easy, Bertrand, engineer and stockholder. Men, even those who best serve idealism, never resist the sensuous temptations of progress. If on the one hand, at the gates of Jaffa, the very caravan of the Queen of Sheba, with its elephants and wild asses, banners and lyres, heralds crowned with anemones, and all its baggage loaded with precious stones and balms, boundless in poetry and legend, were offered to a man of the nineteenth century to bring him slowly to Jerusalem and to Solomon, and, on the other hand, a train whistling along with open windows promised him the same trip with no hot sun or jolting, at fifteen miles per hour and a roundtrip ticket, that man, no matter how intellectual or eruditely artistic he was, would grab his hatbox and greedily board the coach, where he would take off his boots and doze belly up.

Therefore, your malignant work will prosper by virtue of its very malignancy. And in a few years the positive man from the West, who in the morning leaves ancient Joppa in his first-class coach, buys a copy of the *Liberal Gazette of Sinai* at the Gaza station, and has a pleasant meal at the Grand Hotel of the Maccabees in Ramla, will arrive at night in Jerusalem over the Via Dolorosa lighted by electricity to drink a bock and play some billiards at the Holy Sepulcher Casino.

This will be your doing—and the end of the Christian legend.

Goodbye, monster!

Fradique

XII

To Madame de Jouarre
(Transl.)

RAFALDES ESTATE (MINHO)

My dear Godmother,

I am living off the fat of the land in ecclesiastical domains, because this estate once belonged to monks. Now it belongs to a friend who is, like Virgil, a poet and a tiller of the soil, who piously sings of the heroic origins of Portugal as he cultivates his fields and fattens his cattle. Erect, healthy, and tanned by the sun, he has eight children with whom he has populated these monastic cells lined with bright cretonnes. And I have returned to these northern fields of grain from Lisbon precisely to stand as godfather to his latest, a fine little gentleman, three hands tall, the color of brick, all twisting and turning, with a bald head like a melon, small eyes flashing like mirrors among the wrinkles, and a profoundly old skeptical air. On Saturday, Saint Bernard's Day, under a blue sky that Saint Bernard had turned especially bright and soft, to the tolling of clear bells, among the aromas of roses and jasmines, there we carried him, all decorated with ribbons and lace, to the font where Father Teotónio washed away completely the crust of Original Sin covering him from his heels to his small cranium, poor little two-foot long monster who hadn't even had a chance to live his soul and now had lost it . . . And after that, as if Rafaldes were the Land of the Lotus Eaters and I had eaten a lotus blossom instead of cauliflower from the kitchen garden, I've remained here, having forgotten the world and myself in the sweetness of these breezes, these meadows, and all this rural serenity, which caresses me and lulls me to sleep.

The monastic mansion we live in and where the Canons Regular of Saint Augustine, rich and well-fed members of the congregation of the Holy Cross of Coimbra, came to take their ease in summer, is attached by a cloister with blooming hydrangeas to a plain and simple church with an entrance shaded by chestnut trees, thoughtful and grave, as those in the Minho region always are. There is a stone cross over the portal from which the ancient and slow monastic bell still hangs on its iron chain. In the center of the courtyard is the fountain, with good water and chanting drowsily as it falls from basin to basin, and on top there is another stone cross cloaked in a yellowish moss of age-old melancholy. Farther off, in a wide pool, a domestic lake surrounded by benches, where surely the good friars came in the afternoons to drink in coolness and repose, the water for irrigation pours out clear and bountiful below the feet of a stone statue, stiff in her niche, who may be Saint Rita. Still farther on, in the garden, a fragile saint holding a broken vase in her hands presides like a naiad over the bubbling of another fountain, which flows through some granite flumes, sparkling and fleeting, through the bean patch. On the stone supports that hold up the vines here and there a cross or a sacred heart or the monograph of Jesus is engraved. The whole estate, sanctified in that way by holy emblems, recalls a sacristy where the roofs are of grape leaves, the floor is covered with grass, a spring bubbles up through each crack, and incense comes from the carnations.

But in spite of these sacred emblems there is nothing that moves us or harshly pulls us into any renunciation of the world. The estate has always been, as it is now, a place of great plenty, all in food-bearing fields, well-cultivated and well-watered, fertile, lying under the sun like the belly of an ancient nymph. The excellent friars who lived here had a great love for the land and for life. They were noblemen doing service in the militia of the Lord, just as their elder brothers were doing service in the militia of the king, and who, like them, cheerfully enjoyed the leisure, the privileges, and the wealth of their order and their caste. They would come to Rafaldes, during the sultry days of July, in coaches with lackeys. The kitchen was visited more often than the church and every day there were golden capons roasting on the spit. A thin coat of dust veiled the library, where only from time to time would some canon with rheumatism and confined to the cushions of his cell send for a *Don Quixote* or the *Farsas de Dona Petronilla*. Dusted off and well catalogued, with notes and labels in the erudite hand of the abbots—only the wine cellar . . .

In this dwelling of monks, then, you mustn't look for the precious savor of monastic sadness, or the ravines of wood and valley, so barren and silent and so gentle for sustaining in them longings for Heaven, or the thick woods where Saint Bernard became entangled because he found in them a "fruitful silence" more easily than in his cell, or the clearings with pine trees and naked rocks, just right for a hermit's hut and cross . . . No. Here, around the courtyard (where the water of the fountain still runs at the foot of the cross), there are solid granaries for seeds, cozy barns where the cattle fatten, coops with capons and reverend turkeys. Farther on is the lush kitchen garden, fragrant, succulent, and quite sufficient to fill the pots and pans of an entire village, more adorned than a flower garden, with pathways that the strawberry patches border and perfume and to which the trellises give shade, topped as they are by a dense growth of grape leaves. After that comes the threshing floor of clean, smooth granite, sturdily built for long centuries of harvests, with its granary alongside, ventilated, well-aired, so wide that sparrows fly through it as if it were a piece of sky. And, finally, on rich and rolling land, up to the gentle hills, the fields of corn and rye, the low vineyards, the olive groves, the plots of grass, the flax above the streamlets, the flowering grazing land for the livestock . . . Saint Francis of Assisi and Saint Bruno would have abhorred this monastic retreat and would have fled from it as from a living sin.

The interior of the house offers the same worldly comfort. The spacious cells, with paneled ceilings, open onto the planted land and receive from it through the sun-filled windows a perennial feeling of plenty, of rustic opulence, of worldly goods that do not deceive. And the best room, laid out for the most pleasant occupations, is the refectory, with its wide porches where the pampered monks could sip after-dinner coffee, joking, belching, breathing in the coolness, or following the resonant song of a thrush in the beech trees in the yard.

So there was no need to change this dwelling when it passed from religious to secular hands. It was already quite wisely prepared for the profane, and the life that began to be lived in it then was no different from that of the former monastery, just more beautiful, because, free of the contradictions between the spiritual and the temporal, the harmony became perfect. And, such as it is, it slips along with incomparable gentleness. At dawn the cocks crow, the farm awakens, the cattle dogs are tied up, the milkmaid begins milking the cows, the shepherd tosses his crook over his shoulder, the file of farm workers heads out to the fields, and work begins, that work which in Portugal has the marks of the most reliable happiness and an untiring festival because it is accompanied by constant singing. The voices come, loud and rough, cutting into the gentle silence, from the far-off wheat fields or garden plots being hoed, where the whiteness of raw linen shirts stands out and long-fringed kerchiefs shine redder than poppies. And in this work there is neither burden nor speed. All is done with the calmness with which bread ripens in the sun. The plow, rather than cutting the sod, caresses the earth. The rye falls lovingly by itself under the captivating sweep of the scythe. The water knows where the soil is thirsty and there it runs, babbling and sparkling. Ceres in these blessed lands, just as she was in Latium, is the true Goddess of the Earth, propitious and supportive. She gives strength to the laborer's arm, renders his sweat refreshing, and cleanses his soul of all dark cares. Those who serve her, therefore, maintain a happy serenity in the most arduous task. That was the happy pattern of ancient life.

The main meal is at one o'clock and it is serious and full. The whole farm is prodigal with what it furnishes, and the wine, the oil, the vegetables, and the fruit have a richer and healthier taste, having fallen right from the hands of the good Lord onto the table, without passing through markets or stores. In no palace, anywhere, in this over-cultivated Europe does one truly dine as delight-fully as on these rural estates of Portugal. In the smoky kitchen, where there are two earthen pots over four logs burning in the hearth, these village housewives, sleeves rolled up, are cooking a banquet that would have been a jubilation for old Jupiter, that almighty glutton brought up on nectar and the god who ate more and knew how to eat more nobly ever since there were gods in heaven and on earth. Anyone who has never tasted this rice casserole, this Paschal lamb roasted simply on a spit, these chicken giblets as ancient as the monarchy, which fill a person's soul, can never really come to know what that special good fortune was, so crude and so divine, which in the time of the monks was called *tucking in*. And afterwards the farm, with its trellises of deep shade, the sleep-inducing whisper of the irrigating water, the light and dark golden waves of the wheat fields, offers, more than any other human or biblical paradise, just the right kind of rest for someone who has emerged, heavy and content, from that rice and that lamb.

If these noontimes are a bit material, the afternoon will soon bring the por-tion of poetry that the spirit needs. All across the sky the golden glow, the ar-rogant splendor that will not allow itself to be gazed upon and almost repels a person, has been extinguished; now, calm and approachable, it spreads out a softness, a peace that penetrates the soul, makes it also peaceful and soft, and brings about that moment in which sky and soul fraternize and understand each other. The groves rest in an immobility of intelligent contemplation. In the quick trill of the birds there is the retiring awareness of a happy nest. The cattle are returning, single file, from the pastures, weary and full, and go to drink at the cistern, where the dripping of the water under the cross is now lazier. The bells toll the call for the Ave Maria and in all quarters there is the murmur of the name of the Lord. A late cart, loaded down with brushwood, moans along in the shade of the narrow path. And everything is so calm and simple and ten-der, my Godmother, that on any stone bench where I might come to sit I am carried away, feeling the penetrating goodness of things and so much in har-mony with it that there is no thought in this soul, so encrusted with the filth of the world, that couldn't be told to a saint . . .

These afternoons really do sanctify a person. The world withdraws far away, beyond the pine groves and the hills, like some forgotten misery, and then we are truly in the happiness of a monastery with no rules and no abbot, made up only of a natural religiosity that enwraps us, so appropriate for a prayer that has no words and is therefore the one best understood by God.

Then darkness falls and there are fireflies in the hedges. Venus, tiny, glitters on high. The parlor above is filled with books, books that remained closed in the time of the monks—for this house has become spiritualized since it no longer belongs to a religious order. And the day on the estate comes to an end with slow and quiet conversation about ideas and letters, while one of Portugal's fados, heavy with longing and laments, moans on the Portuguese guitar, and the moon, a red full moon, rises beyond the balcony, as if hearkening from behind the dark hills.

Deus nobis haec otia fecit in umbra Lusitaniae pulcherrimae . . .[28] Bad Latin, grateful truth.

Your grateful and bad Godson,

Fradique

XIII

To Clara . . .
(Transl.)
PARIS, NOVEMBER

My love,

Just a few moments ago (ten moments, ten minutes, which I spent in the desolation of a fiacre carrying me from our Ivory Tower) I was still feeling the beating of your heart next to mine, with nothing separating them except a bit of human clay, so beautiful in you, so coarse in me, and I am already trying anxiously, with this lifeless piece of paper, to pick up again that ineffable *being with you* that today is the aim of my whole life, my supreme and only life. The fact is that away from your presence I cease living, things stop existing for me, and I am left like a dead man lying in the middle of a dead world. So therefore, as soon as I see the end of those perfect and brief moments of life that you give me, by simply sitting down beside me and whispering my name, I begin again to pine desperately for you as for a resurrection.

Before loving you, before receiving my Eve from the hands of my God, what was I really? A shadow drifting among shadows. But you came along, my sweet adored one, to make me feel my reality and let me too shout triumphantly my *"amo, ergo sum!"*[29] And it wasn't just my reality that you revealed to me, but also the reality of this whole universe, which had me encased in an unintelligible and gray pile of appearances. When a few days ago, at dusk, on the terrace in

Savran, you complained that I was gazing at the stars when your eyes were right beside me and that I watched the sleeping hills next to the warmth of your shoulders, you didn't know nor did I know then how to explain to you that my contemplation was simply a new way still of adoring you, because I was really admiring in things the unexpected beauty that you pour over them with an emanation that belongs to you and which, before living alongside you, I had never perceived in them, just as one doesn't perceive the red of the roses or the gentle green of the meadows before sunrise. It was you, my beloved, who lighted up the world for me. In your love I had my initiation. I understand now, I know now. And, like an ancient initiate, I can state, "I, too, went to Eleusis; along the highway I hanged many flowers that were not real, before many altars that were not divine; but I reached Eleusis, I entered Eleusis, and I saw and felt the truth! . . ."

And what is more, for my martyrdom and glory, you are so sumptuously beautiful and so ethereally beautiful, with a beauty made of heaven and earth, a complete beauty, and only yours, one I had already conceived of but which I never judged could be realized. How many times, standing before that always admired and always perfect Venus de Milo, have I thought that if under her brow of a goddess there had been a tumult of human woes; if her sovereign and mute eyes had known the overlay of tears; if her lips, carved only for honey and for kisses, had let themselves tremble with the whisper of a submissive plea; if under those breasts, which had been the sublime appetite of gods and heroes, love had throbbed one day and with it goodness; if her marble had suffered and through suffering had become spiritualized, joining to her splendor and harmony the grace of fragility; if she were of our time and felt our ills and, while still the Goddess of Pleasure, became the Lady of Sorrows—then she would not have been placed in a museum but consecrated in a shrine, because men, as they recognized in her the always coveted and always frustrated alliance of the real and the ideal, would certainly have acclaimed her *in aeternum* as the definitive divinity.[30] But to what avail? Poor Venus offered only the serene magnificence of the flesh. She lacked entirely the flame that burns in the soul and consumes it. And the incomparable creature of my pondering, the spiritual Venus, Citherea and Dolorosa, didn't exist, would never exist . . . And as I was thinking like that, behold, you rose up and I understood you! You were the incarnation of my dream, or, rather, of a dream that must be a universal one—but only I discovered you, or only I was so lucky that you wished to be discovered by me!

See, then, how I shall never let you escape my arms. For that very reason, that you are my Divinity forever and are irrevocably the prisoner of my adoration. The priests of Carthage attached images of their Baals to the pavement of the temples with bronze chains. I want you that way too, chained inside the greedy temple I have built for you, my only divinity, always at your altar—as I am always before it on my hands and knees, constantly receiving your visitation in my soul, ceaselessly losing myself in your essence, so that not for a moment will there be any break in that ineffable fusion, which for you is an act of mercy and for me an act of salvation. What I would really like is for you to be invisible to everyone, as though you didn't exist, with a shapeless covering to hide your body, a strict muteness to conceal your intelligence. In that way you would pass through the world as an incomprehended shadow. And only for me would your dazzling perfection be revealed inside that dark wrapping. Just see how much I love you that I should want you enwrapped in a simple, vague, woolen garment, with a silent, inanimate appearance . . . In that way I would lose the triumphal contentment of seeing, resplendent among the marveling multitude, the one who secretly loves me. Everyone would whisper with compassion, "Poor thing!" And only I would know about the adorable body and soul of the "poor thing."

How adorable! Nor can I understand how, aware of your charms, you are not in love with yourself, like that Narcissus who trembles with the cold and is covered with moss on the edge of the fountain in Savran. But I love you broadly, both for me and for *you*! Your beauty truly attains the height of a virtue and it must have been the so very pure ways of your soul that sketched the so very beautiful lines of your body. For that reason I have in me an incessant despair of not knowing how to love you worthily, or, rather (since you have descended from a higher heaven), of not knowing how to treat and serve the divine guest in my heart as she deserves to be treated and served. Sometimes I would like to enfold you completely in an immaterial, seraphic happiness, as infinitely calm as blissful contentment should be—and in that way we could slip along, arm in arm, through the silence and the light, very softly, in a dream filled with certainty, leaving life at the same time and continuing on in the *beyond* with the same ecstatic dream. And at other times I would like to transport you into a vehement, tumultuous, blazing happiness, all in flames, so that we would be sublimely destroyed in it and all that would be left of us would be a bit of ash, with no memory and no name! I have an old print of a Satan, still in all the brilliance of his archangelic beauty, dragging toward the Abyss a nun, a saint, whose last veils of penitence are being torn by the tips of the black rocks. And on the face of the saint, through the horror, there shines, unrepressed and stronger than the horror, a joy and passion so intense that I would love to see them in you, oh my stolen saint! But in none of these ways do I know how to love you, so weak and clumsy is my heart, so that since my love is not perfect I must content myself with its being eternal. You smile sadly at this eternity. You asked me only yesterday, "In the calendar of your heart, how many days does eternity last?" But consider that I was a corpse and you brought me back to life. The new blood that circulates in my veins, the new spirit that feels and understands in me, are my love for you and if it were to run away from me, I would have to once again, ice cold and mute, return to my tomb. I can only cease loving you when I cease to be. And life with you and for you is so inexpressively beautiful! It is the life of a god. Even better perhaps. And if I were that pagan you say I am, but a pagan from Latium, a shepherd, a believer still in Jupiter and Apollo, I would be afraid that at any moment one of those envious gods would steal you away and take you up to Olympus to fulfill his divine happiness. I'm not afraid of that. I know you're all mine, forever and for all. I look at the world around us as a paradise created just for us and I sleep securely in your breast in the fullness of glory, oh, my thrice blessed one, Queen of my Grace!

Do not think that I am composing canticles in your praise. I am simply releasing what is bubbling up inside my soul . . . Quite the contrary, all the poetry from all the ages, with all its grace and majesty, would be impotent to express my ecstasy. I am babbling out my infinite prayer as best I can. And in this desolating insufficiency of human speech, it is like the most uneducated and unlettered person that I kneel before you, lift my hands, and promise you the only truth, better than all truths, that I love you, and I love you, and I love you, and I love you! . . .

Fradique

XIV
To Madame de Jouarre
(Transl.)
LISBON, JUNE

My dear Godmother,

In that boarding house on the Travessa da Palha where, yoked to his anguished work on the truth, my cousin the metaphysician lives, right after I got back from Rafaldes, I met a priest, a Father Salgueiro, whom you, with that malicious patience of yours for collecting types, might find interesting and psychologically amusing.

My inattentive and pale metaphysician finds, with a shrug of his shoulders, that Father Salgueiro doesn't stand out in any particular way either in body or soul among the vague priests of his diocese and that he even represents summarily, in a manner as faithful as an index, the thinking, the feelings, the life, and the appearance of the whole ecclesiastical class in Portugal. As a matter of fact, seen outside his shell, Father Salgueiro is the usual and current Portuguese priest, raised on a farm, tamed and refined afterwards by the seminary, by contact with the authorities and secretariats, by links from the confessional and Masses with noble ladies who own chapels, and, above all, by long residences in Lisbon in these boarding houses in the Baixa, infested with literature and politics. Deep breathing has made him barrel-chested, like a bellows of a forge. His hands are still dark and rough in spite of long contact with the whiteness and softness of the Host. The skin on his face is the color of tanned hide, with an overtone of blue on his close-shaven jaws. His tonsure stands out pale in the midst of hair that is darker and thicker than a horse's mane. His teeth are shamelessly white. Everything about him belongs to those strong agricultural common people from whom he emerged and who in Portugal still today furnish the Church with its personnel, from the desire they have to ally themselves with and lean on the only great human institution that they really understand and don't mistrust. Inside, however, in his marrow, Father Salgueiro presents for someone like me a whole delightfully new and picturesque moral structure of the Lusitanian clergy, which I had only glimpsed from the outside, as a cassock disappearing through the door of a sacristy, an old snuff-stained handkerchief laid on the edge of a confessional, a surplice showing white in a carriage following a corpse.

What charmed me right off about Father Salgueiro, on the night that we chatted so long while we lazily circled the Rossio, was his concept of the priesthood. For him the priesthood (which he clearly loves and reveres as one of the most fundamental tools of society) does not constitute a spiritual function in any way, but only and categorically a civil one. Never since he was appointed to his parish has Father Salgueiro considered himself anything but a functionary of the state, a public employee who wears a uniform, the cassock (just as a customs guard wears a military jacket), and who, instead of going into an office on the Terreiro do Paço every morning to copy and file away documents, goes even on holy days to a different bureau, where instead of a file cabinet an altar stands, there to celebrate mass and administer the sacraments. His relationships, therefore, are not and never have been with Heaven (all he cares to know about heaven is whether or not it will rain) but with the Secretariat of Justice and Ecclesiastical Affairs. They were the ones who placed him in his parish, not to continue the work of the Lord, sweetly guiding men toward the pure road to salvation (missions that are not taken care of by secretariats of the state), but as a functionary who executes certain public acts that the law determines for the good of the social order: baptizing, confessing, marrying, and burying his parishioners.

The sacraments are, therefore, for the excellent Father Salgueiro, mere civil ceremonies, indispensable for the regulation of the civil state, and never since he has been administering them has he thought about their divine nature, the grace that they communicate to souls, or the strength with which they tie this transitory life to an imminent principle. Of course, in past times, in the seminary, Father Salgueiro had learned by heart from greasy textbooks his Dogmatic Theology, his Pastoral Theology, his Morals, his Saint Thomas, and his Liguori, but only so as to fulfill the official requirements of the course, to be ordained by his bishop, and later to be provided with a parish for him to administer, like all the other graduates in Coimbra who memorize the lecture notes in Natural Law and Roman Law in order to "get the degree," receive the doctor's tassel on their caps, and after that the coziness of an easy job. The degree is worth all that matters because it justifies an office. The knowledge is the painful formality that leads one there, a true test which, after one has gone through it, leaves no desire in one's spirit to return to the discipline, to its aridity and its fatigue. Today Father Salgueiro has comfortably forgotten the theological and spiritual meaning of marriage; but he marries people, he marries them expertly, with fine liturgical rigor, with good civil certification, scrupulously examining the documents, placing in his blessing all the prescribed unction, perfect in joining hands under his stole and proper in his Latin, because he is subsidized by the state to marry its citizens well and as a zealous employee he doesn't wish to have any defects in the functions for which he receives timely payment.

His ignorance is delightful. Apart from a few acts in the life of Jesus—the flight into Egypt on donkeyback, the multiplication of the loaves at the marriage feast in Cana, the scourge of the money changers in the Temple, some expulsions of demons—he knows nothing about the Gospels, which he considers *very beautiful*, however. The doctrine of Jesus is as alien to him as is the philosophy of Hegel. Of the Bible, too, he knows only some scattered episodes, which he must have learned from pictures: Noah's Ark, Samson bringing down the gates of Gaza, Judith beheading Holofernes. What also amuses me, on the friendly nights when we chat on the Travessa da Palha, is his absolutely innocent lack of knowledge of the origins of church history. Father Salgueiro imagines that Christianity was founded suddenly one day (a Sunday, of course) by an instantaneous miracle of Jesus Christ. And everything that has occurred since that festive occasion is shrouded for him by an uncertain darkness, broken up here and there by the vague light of saints' halos and popes' tiaras, all the way up to Pius IX. In the pontifical works of Pius IX, however, he admires neither the Infallibility nor the Syllabus, for he prides himself on being a liberal who wants more progress, blesses the benefits of education, and subscribes to *O Primeiro de Janeiro*.

Where I also find him extremely picturesque is when he is chatting about the duties that fall upon him as a shepherd of souls—his duties toward those souls. That he should be obliged, as a continuation of divine work, to console grief, pacify enmities, guide repentant sinners, teach the cultivation of goodness, and soften the demands of selfishness, is for the worthy Father Salgueiro the strangest and most incoherent of novelties! Not that he fails to recognize the moral beauty of that mission, which he even considers one *filled with poetry*, but he will not admit that, beautiful and honorable as it is, it belongs to him, Father Salgueiro. It would be pretty much the same as demanding of a customs checker that he should moralize and purify commerce. That holy undertaking belongs to saints. And saints, in Father Salgueiro's opinion, form a caste, a spiritual aristocracy with supernatural obligations that are delegated to them and paid for by heavens. Quite different are the obligations of a parish priest! An ecclesiastical functionary, he only has to fulfill ritual functions in the name of the Church and, therefore, of the State that subsidizes it. Is there a child to be baptized? Father Salgueiro picks up his stole and baptizes it. Is there a body to be buried? Father Salgueiro picks up his hyssop and buries it. At the end of the month, he receives his ten mil-réis (in addition to alms) and the recognition of his bishop for his zeal.

The idea that Father Salgueiro has of his mission determines his conduct with praiseworthy logic. He gets up at ten o'clock, the classically chosen hour by employees of the state. He never opens his breviary except in the presence of his ecclesiastical superiors, and then out of hierarchical deference, the way, in the presence of his general, a lieutenant comes to attention and places his hand on his sword. As for prayers, meditations, mortification, examination of the soul, all those patient methods of personal perfection and sanctification, he never even suspected that they might be necessary or favorable for him. What for? Father Salgueiro is constantly aware that as a functionary he must maintain, without compromise or omissions, the decorum that will render his functions respected by the world. Therefore, he always dresses in black. He doesn't smoke. On all days of abstinence he austerely dines on fish. He has never crossed the impure threshold of a tavern. In winter, on one night only, he goes to a theater, to the São Carlos, when they are singing *Poliuto*, a sacred opera with a most pure lesson. He would cut off his tongue with ferocity if from it the smallest bit of a lie were to drip. And he is chaste. He doesn't condemn or repel women with wrath like the Holy Fathers. He even venerates them if they are thrifty and virtuous. But the rules of the church prohibit women. He is an ecclesiastical functionary and women, therefore, do not enter into his functions. He is rigidly chaste. I know of no greater respectability than Father Salgueiro's.

His occupations, from what I can observe, are, quite logically for an employee (in addition to the hours given over to his liturgical duties), involved in seeking to better his employment. He belongs therefore to a political party in Lisbon and three nights a week he has tea at the home of its leader, to which he brings along some candy for the ladies. He handles elections skillfully. He performs services and errands, complex and unwritten, for all the directors of the Secretariat of Ecclesiastical Affairs. He is untiring in chores for his bishop and just a few months ago I found him perspiring and afflicted because of two undertakings for His Excellency: one having to do with cheesecakes from Sintra and the other with a collection of the *Diário do Governo*.

I haven't spoken of his intelligence. It is a practical and methodical one, as I was able to verify from listening to a sermon he preached on the feast of Saint Venantius. For that sermon, which had been comissioned, Father Salgueiro received twenty mil-réis and for that price he gave a succulent and documented sermon, containing everything needed for the glorification of Saint Venantius. He established the saint's lineage; he listed all of the saint's miracles (which are few in number) with precision, setting down the dates and citing the authorities; he narrated his martyrdom with hagiological rigor; he listed the churches that have been consecrated to him, along with the periods of their founding. He also skillfully inserted words of praise for the Minister of Ecclesiastical Affairs. Nor did he forget the Royal Family, to whom he rendered constitutional homage. It was, in short, an excellent report on Saint Venantius.

That night I fervently congratulated the Reverend Father Salgueiro. He said, softly, with modesty and simplicity:

"Saint Venantius, unfortunately, isn't all that important. He wasn't a bishop and he never held any public office . . . But, in any case, I think I fulfilled my duty."

I've heard that he's going to be made a canon. He has amply merited this promotion. Jesus couldn't have a better scribe. And I have never really understood why another friend of mine, a friar from Varatojo who, for the ecstasy of his faith, the profusion of his charity, and his overwhelming care for the pacification of souls, reminds me of ancient evangelicals, always refers to this so zealous, so punctual, so proficient, so respectable priest as "that horrible Father Salgueiro"!

Just think of this, then, Godmother. More than thirty or forty thousand years are needed for a mountain to be undone and reduced to a tiny little hillock over which a small goat playfully leaps. And less than two thousand years were enough for Christianity to come down from the great priests of the Seven Churches of Asia to the amusing Father Salgueiro, who doesn't belong to seven churches or even to one but only, and quite devotedly, to the Secretariat of Ecclesiastical Affairs. This tumble would have been enough to prove the fragility of the divine, were it not for the fact that the divine really encompasses religions and mountains, Asia, Father Salgueiro, and the playful little goats, everything that is made and everything that is unmade, even this Godson of yours, who is nevertheless quite human.

Fradique

XV
To Bento de S.
PARIS, OCTOBER

My dear Bento,

Your idea of starting a newspaper is harmful and horrible. By publishing, and in an expensive format, with telegrams and chronicles, another of "those printed sheets that appear every morning," as the Archbishop of Paris so fearfully and chastely says, you will see that in your time and country quick judgments will become only quicker, vanity will become all the sharper, and intolerance will become all the more hardened. Quick judgment, vanity, intolerance—there you have three dark social sins that morally bring on the death of a society. And there you are, merrily preparing to liven them up. Oblivious like the plague, you are spreading death over souls. The Devil is most assuredly adding more coals under the kettle of pitch where after the Final Judgment you will be boiling and howling, my dear Benedictus, my dear reprobate.

Don't think that I'm exaggerating like some bitter moralist, like a Saint John Chrysostom. Consider first how it has unmistakably been the press, with its superficial, flighty, and rash way of affirming everything and judging everything, that has rooted the lethal habit of quick judgments in our time. Over all the centuries, of course, opinions were heedlessly improvised. The Greeks were inconsiderate and garrulous, and Moses, during his long sojourn in the wilderness, suffered the varied gossiping of the Hebrews. But never, as it has in our hurried century, did that impudent improvisation become the natural method for understanding something. With the exception of a few philosophers enslaved by method and a few devout people gnawed at by scruples, today we have all become unaccustomed to or, rather, rid ourselves happily of the arduous task of verification. It is with fleeting impressions that we form our firm conclusions. In order to judge the most complex fact in politics, we content ourselves with a rumor we happened to hear on a street corner on some windy morning. In literature, in order to make an appreciation of the densest book, brimming with new ideas that loving care had firmly developed and connected over long years, all that we deem necessary is to leaf through a page here and there in a darkening cloud of cigar smoke. Especially in the act of condemning, our lightness is ruthless. With such sovereign ease do we declare, "This is a piece of garbage! The man's a charlatan!" We put up a more considered resistance to declaring, "He's a genius!" or "He's a saint!" But even then, when the digestion of a good meal or the soft light of a May sky inclines us toward benevolence, we wildly concede, and with only a quick glance at the elected one, a crown or a halo for him, and with that we advance the popularity of some rascal now decorated with laurels or a gleaming aureole. That's how we spend our blessed days, stamping defining labels on the backs of men and things. There's no act, individual or collective, personality, or human work upon where we're not quick roundly to promulgate a nice, fat opinion. And the opinion always and only has as its basis that tiny little bit of fact of the man or the work that passed in a flash before our slippery and casual eyes. By a gesture we judge a character and by a character we judge a people. An Englishman with whom in times past I traveled through Asia, a respectable man, a learned collaborator in scholarly journals, a member of Academies, considered all Frenchmen, from senators to sweepers, to be "pigs and thieves." Why, my dear Bento? Because his father-in-law's house had had a valet who may have come from Dijon and who never changed his collar and pilfered cigars. This Englishman is a masterful illustration of the scandalous formation of our generalizations.

And who has rooted these habits of desolating superficiality in us? Newspapers, the newspapers which every morning give us, from news items to advertisements, a frothy mass of superficial judgments improvised the night before, at midnight, in the midst of the hissing of the gas and the bubbling of the banter, by fine young fellows who storm through the editorial rooms, grab a sheet of paper, and without even taking off their hats make decisions about everything between heaven and earth with two scratches of their pens. Whether it's a question of a national revolution, the solidity of a bank, a magic show, or a derailment, the tip of the pen with one scribble spills it out and passes judgment. No study, no documentation, no proof. Just last Sunday, my dear Bento, a distinguished newspaper in Paris, commenting on the economic and political situation in Portugal, stated, and with upright knowledge, that "in Lisbon the sons of the most illustrious families of the aristocracy are working as *porters at the customhouse* and at the end of each month send *their servants* to pick up their wages"! What do you have to say about the heirs to the historic houses of Portugal loading barrels of olive oil on the customhouse docks and keeping liveried servants to go pick up their wages? These barrels, these noblemen, these lackeys of the stevedores make up a delightful and chimerical customhouse that isn't so much out of *The Thousand and One Nights* as from the Thousand and One Jackasseries. Well, this is what was taught by an important newspaper, wealthy and well provided with encyclopedias, maps, statistics, telephones, and telegraph lines, with a very erudite and handsomely paid staff who know Europe, belong to the Academy of Moral and Social Sciences, and legislate in the Senate! And you, Bento, in your paper, also furnished with encyclopedias and telephones, with your pen in unrestrained motion, will deliver about France and China, and the unlucky universe that becomes your subject matter and property, judgments just as solid and as proven as those which that other blessed newspaper has filed, so definitively, about our customhouse and our nobility . . .

This is the first sin, and quite a dark one. Now consider another that's even darker. Through the newspaper and its reporting, which will be its function and its strength, you will develop in your time and in your land all the evils of vanity. Reporting, I know very well, is a useful supplier of history. It certainly mattered knowing whether Cleopatra's nose was curved or flat because for a long time, from Philippi to Actium, the destiny of the universe depended on the shape of that nose. And think of all the many details that reporters' penetrating gossip reveals about Mr. Renan and his furniture and his underwear, all those positive elements that the twentieth century will need to reconstruct with certainty the personality of the author of *The Origins of Christianity* and through it understand the work. But the way that reporting is practiced today, there is less about those who influence the business of the world or the direction of its thought than, as the Bible says, about all the "fortune and conditions of the vain," from jockeys to murderers. This indiscriminate publicity has little to do with the documentation of history and very much, prodigiously and scandalously, with propagation of vanities!

Newspapers are, in fact, the tireless bellows that blow air on human vanity, prodding and enhancing its flame. It has existed all through the ages, man's vanity! A mournful Solomon lamented it and Alcibiades, the greatest of the Greeks perhaps, was lost because of it. But without any doubt, my dear Bento, never has vanity been, as it is in our cursed nineteenth century, the puffing engine of thought and conduct. In these civilized states, loud and hollow, everything derives from vanity, everything inclines toward vanity. And the new form of vanity for the civilized person consists in having his fine name printed in the newspaper, his fine person commented on in the newspaper. *To get my name in the paper*! There you have today's impatient aspiration and supreme recompense. In aristocratic regimes one's effort was aimed at obtaining, if not the favor, at least the smile of a prince. In our democracies the anxiety of the majority of mortals is to attain seven lines of praise in the newspaper. In order to conquer those seven blessed lines men will practice all manner of actions, even good ones. Even good ones, my dear Bento! "Our generous friend Z . . ." only sends his hundred mil-réis to the foundling home so that the papers will exalt the hundred mil-réis of our generous friend Z . . . Nor must the seven lines contain a great deal of honey and incense. It's sufficient for them just to make one's name appear in nice, black letters, the glow of which is more appetizing than the golden halo of the old days of sainthood. And no class is exempt from being devoured by that morbid hunger for fame. It gnaws as much at people of superficiality and worldliness as it does at those who only seem to love in life, as its best form, peace and quiet . . . We are entering Lent now (it is among the ashes and with the ashes that I am moralizing for you). During these weeks of fish, the Dominican friars are deafening with their preaching from the depths of their cloisters and the pulpits of Paris. And why do they preach such sensational sermons, with their profane and theatrical art, their displays of amorous psychology, affectations of evangelical anarchism, and so creative of scandals that Paris runs more greedily to Notre Dame on afternoons of the Dominicans than to the Comédie Française on a night with Coquelin? Because the monks, the sons of Saint Dominic, want their seven lines in the newspapers on the Boulevard and all the fame that actors receive. The newspaper stretches out all over the world its two pages, speckled with black, just like the two wings with which iconographers of the fifteenth century used to represent Extravagance and Greed, and the whole world rushes out to the newspaper, wants to crouch under the two wings that will lift it up to false glory and spread its name through the resounding air. And it is for that false glory that men lose themselves, women debase themselves, politicians dismantle the order of the state, artists prance about in aesthetic extravagance, learned men show off ridiculous theories, and from every corner, in every field, the howling horde of charlatans rises up . . . (How pompous and loud I am sounding . . . !) But it's true, my dear Bento. Just look at the number of people who prefer being insulted to being ignored. (Petty men of letters, lady poets, dentists, etc.) The evil itself relishes being talked about in the seven lines that curse it. In order to appear in the newspaper there are murderers who commit murder. Even the old instinct of self-preservation yields to the new instinct of notoriety, and there is the wretch who at a funeral that has been converted into an apotheosis by the number of wreaths, coaches, and oratorical plaints will lick his lips thoughtfully and wish he could be the corpse.

This summer, quite early one morning, I went into a tavern in Montmartre to buy some matches. At the zinc-covered bar, over two glasses of white wine, was a vagrant, who, from his flat nose, his bushy, drooping mustache, and his otter-skin cap, looked like (and was) a Hun, a survivor of the hordes of Alaric, shouting to another drifter who was pale and beardless and at whom he was shoving a newspaper:

"There it is, all written out in letters, my whole name! In the second column, right at the top, where it says, 'Yesterday an infamous, vile bandit . . .' That's me! My whole name!"

And he slowly spread his look of triumph out over the place. There you have, as it is put nowadays so affectedly, a fine "state of the soul"! You, Bento, will be creating those states.

So, then, just consider the final and darkest sin. With your newspaper you will be founding a new school of intolerance. You will be erecting around yourself, your party, and your friends a small and firmly cemented wall. Inside that little wall, on which you plant your banner with the usual motto of *impartiality, disinterest, etc.*, there will only be, according to Bento and his newspaper, intelligence, dignity, wisdom, energy, and civility; outside, according to Bento's paper, there will only be, necessarily, folly, villainy, inertia, selfishness, and rascality. It is party discipline (and so as not to displease you, by party I mean party in its broadest sense, taking in literature, philosophy, etc.) that inevitably imposes on you that amusing separation of virtues and vices. Once you have entered into battle you will never be able to admit that reason or justice or utility can be found on the side of those against whom you are firing off in the morning your whistling shrapnel of adjectives and verbs, because then decency, if not conscience, would force you to leap over the wall and desert to the side of those just people. You must sustain the idea that they are malevolent, unreasoning knaves who fully deserve the lead you are piercing them with. From the soles of your feet to the sparse hairs on your head, you immediately become bogged down in intolerance, my dear Bento. Any idea that arises on the other side of the wall you will condemn as a disaster without examining it at all, simply because it has appeared ten yards away, on the side of those other people, who are the reprobates, and not on the side of your people, who are the elect. Have those others produced a work of some kind? Bento will spare no words or efforts to see that it perishes, and if through the stones he is casting at it he happens to catch sight of a spot of beauty or utility, he will furiously speed up its demolition because it would be mortifying for his friends if something of use or beauty should be born from their enemies and were to go on living. In the men who are wandering about beyond your wall you will see only sinners; and if you recognized among them Saint Francis of Assisi distributing the last farthings of Porziuncola among the poor, you would cover your eyes so that all that holiness wouldn't soften you and you would shout with redoubled wrath, "There goes that good-for-nothing wasting the money he stole on vagrants!"

That's what it will be like with you and your newspaper. And all around you those who buy it and follow its lead will slowly and morally take on your image. The whole newspaper will distill intolerance the way an alembic distills alcohol, and every morning the masses poison themselves with swallows of that insidious venom. It is through the actions of newspapers that all the old conflicts in the world are exacerbated, while souls are disevangelized and become more rebellious against tolerance. Incessant sociability has softened and smoothed human divergences, the way a river softens and smoothes the pebbles that roll along with it, and humanity, which long-surviving culture and old age have turned pleasantly sociable, would go on ahead toward a supreme peacefulness if every morning the newspaper didn't arouse the hatreds of principles, classes, and races, and with its shouting didn't incite them, the way mastiffs are goaded into a fury that makes them bite. The newspaper today fulfills all the malignant functions of the defunct Satan, from whom it has inherited his ubiquity, and it is not only the Father of Lies but also the Father of Discord. It is the one who, on the one side, inflames the most voracious demands and, on the other, furnishes the brick and mortar for the most iniquitous resistances. Just see how when a strike breaks out, or when the interests of two nations suddenly clash, or when in the spiritual sphere two credos confront each other with hostility, the first instinct of men, whom the rub of material civilization has softened and demartialized, is to say softly *peace!*, *reason!*, and to hold out their hands to each other in that hereditary gesture which is the basis of pacts. But the newspaper immediately rises up, irritated like the ancient Fury, separating them and blowing intransigence into their souls, pushing them into battle and filling the air with tumult and dust.

The newspaper killed the peace of the land. And not only does it stir up already dormant questions like embers in a fireplace, until a furious flame leaps up again, but it also invents new dissensions, like that nascent anti-Semitism that before the century ends will repeat the anachronistic and brutal medieval persecutions. And it is also the newspaper . . .

But hark! Eleven o'clock! Eleven nimble hours are dancing Glück's minuet in my old clock. This letter is on its way now, like that of Tiberius, quite thunderous and verbose, *verbosa et tremenda epistola*, and I am in a hurry to end it so I may go before lunch to read my newspapers, with delight.

Always yours,

Fradique

XVI

To Clara . . .

(Transl.)

PARIS, OCTOBER

My beloved Clara,

All wrapped up in complaints, almost sullen and mentally clothed in mourning, your letter appeared today with the first chills of October. And why, my sweet unhappy one? Because, more cruel-hearted than a Trastámara or a Borgia, I have been five days (five short autumn days) without sending you a line affirming that ever so patent truth and as well known to you as the disc of the sun, "That I think only of you and live only in you! . . ." But don't you know, my super-beloved, that your memory throbs in my soul as naturally and as perennially as the blood in my heart? What other principle governs and maintains my life if not your love? Do you still really need a certificate every morning, stating in bold letters that my passion is alive and well and sends you a *Good morning*? What for? To calm your uncertainty? Good Heavens! Might it not be, rather, as a gift to your pride? You know that you are a Goddess and you demand incessant incense and canticles from your worshipper. But your patron Saint Clara was a great saint, of high lineage, of triumphal beauty, the friend of Saint Francis of Assisi, the confidante of Pope Gregory IX, the founder of convents, the gentle fount of piety and miracles—and yet she is only fêted once a year, on the 27th of August.

You know quite well that I am only teasing you, Saint Clara of my faith. No! I haven't sent you that superfluous line because all kinds of ills have suddenly fallen upon me: a burlesque catarrh, along with melancholy, obtuseness, and sneezes; a confused duel in which I was the weary second and in which only the dry branch of a tree was wounded, cut by a bullet; and, finally, someone just back from Abyssinia, cruelly abyssiniating, to whom I had to listen with resigned amazement as he went on about caravans, dangers, loves, exploits, and lions . . . And there you have how my poor Clara, all alone in her forests, has been without this leaf covered with my writing and as useless in its assurance of her heart as the leaves that surround her, withered now, certainly, and dancing in the wind.

Yet, I don't know how the leaves in your forest behave, but here the leaves in my poor garden have yellowed and are rolling about on the damp grass. In order to console myself for the loss of the greenery, I lit a fire in my fireplace and all last night I buried myself in the very old chronicle of a scribe from my country named Fernão Lopes. In it he tells of a king who was given the weak name of *The Handsome* and who, because of a great love, disdained princesses of Castile and Aragon, dissipated treasuries, faced sedition, suffered the dissatisfaction of his people, lost the vassalage of castles and lands, and almost brought down his kingdom! I was already familiar with the chronicle, but only now do I understand the king. And I envy him greatly, my beautiful Clara. When someone loves as he did (or as I do), it must be a splendid contentment to have princesses of Christendom and treasuries and a people and a strong kingdom to sacrifice for two delicate and languid eyes, smiling at what they expect and even more for what they promise . . . One should really only love when one is a king, for only then can one prove the height of his feelings with the magnificence of his sacrifice. But a mere vassal like me (with no hosts or castle), what does he possess of wealth, nobility, or beauty to sacrifice? Time, fortune, life? Of scant worth. It's like offering a handful of dust. And then his beloved will not even remain in history.

And, as for history, I approve very much, my studious Clara, of your reading that of the divine Buddha. You say, disconsolately, that to you he only seems to be a *very complicated Jesus*. But, my love, you must disentangle that poor Buddha from the heavy flood of legends and miracles that the imagination of Asia has loaded him down with over the centuries. Just the way it was, devoid of its mythology and in its historical nudity, a better soul has never visited the earth, and nothing can equal in heroic virtue the night of the Great Renunciation. Jesus was a proletarian, a beggar with neither vineyard nor garden plot, with no terrestrial love, who wandered through the fields of Galilee advising men to abandon, as he had, their home and possessions, to descend to the solitude of a mendicant in order one day to enter a venturesome, abstract kingdom in the sky. He sacrificed nothing himself and he instigated others into sacrifice, calling upon all the high and mighty to come down to the level of his humbleness. The Buddha, on the other hand, was a prince, and, as they are accustomed to be in Asia, of unlimited power and unlimited wealth. He married out of an immense love and from that there came to him a son in whom that love became sublime. And that prince, that husband, that father, one day, out of dedication to mankind, leaves his palace, his kingdom, his beloved spouse, his little son asleep in a cradle made of mother-of-pearl, and in the crude, rough woolen garb of a beggar goes out into the world asking for alms and preaching the renunciation of pleasures, the annihilation of all desires, the limitless love for living creatures, an incessant perfection through charity, a strong disdain for the asceticism that tortures, the perennial cultivation of a piety that redeems and a confidence in death . . .

Unquestionably, in my eyes (as far as these noble matters can be discerned in a house in Paris in the nineteenth century and with a cold), the life of the Buddha is much more meritorious. And consider also the difference in the teachings of the two divine Masters. One, Jesus, says, "I am the son of God and I urge each one of you mortal men to practice good during the few years that you spend on this earth so that later on, as a reward, I can give each of you individually a superior existence, infinite in years and infinite in delights, in a palace that is beyond the clouds and which is that of my Father!" The Buddha says simply, "I am a poor mendicant monk and I beg of you to be good during life because from you, in recompense, others better will be born, and of them others even more perfect, and thus, with the increased practice of virtue with each generation, universal virtue will gradually be established on earth!" Therefore, the justice of the just according to Jesus only works selfishly to the advantage of the just. But the justice of the just according to the Buddha works to the advantage of the being whose existence follows his, and then to another born of him, down throughout their passage on earth for the eternal reward of the earth. Jesus creates an aristocracy of saints, whom he carries off to Heaven where he is king and where they will make up the heavenly court for the pleasure of his divinity; and no direct advantage comes of this to the world, which continues to suffer its portion of evil, always undiminished. The Buddha creates, through the sum of individual virtues accumulated in a saintly way, a humanity that, with each cycle, is born progressively better and which in the end will become perfect and extend itself all over the earth, where evil will disappear and where the Buddha will always be, by the side of the rough road, the same mendicant friar. I, my flower, stand with the Buddha. In any case, those two Masters possessed, for the good of mankind, the greatest portion of divinity that up till now has ever been given the human soul to contain. Moreover, all of this is rather complicated and you would proceed wisely in leaving the Buddha to his Buddhism and, seeing how admirable are those forests of yours, let their strength and their healthful aromas fortify you. The Buddha belongs to the city and to the Collège de France. In the country, real knowledge should fall from the trees, as in the time of Eve. Any elm leaf can teach you more than all the leaves in books. Especially more than I can, as I go on pontificating here and pedantically offering before your lovely eyes, so fair and soft, a scandalous course in Comparative Religions.

I only have three more inches of space left and I still haven't given you, oh my sweet exile, the news of Paris, *Acta Urbis*. (Lord, now it's Latin, no less!) There's not much and it's pale. It's raining. We're still a Republic. Madame de Jouarre, who got back from Rocha with fewer gray hairs but crueler, invited a few unfortunates (of whom I was the greatest) to listen to three chapters of a new assault on Greece by the Baron de Fernay. The newspapers have published another preface by Mr. Renan, all full of Mr. Renan, and in which he shows himself to be, as always, the sensitive and erudite vicar of Our Lady of Reason. And we have, finally, a marriage of passion and luxury, that of our sculptural Viscount de Fomblant to Mademoiselle Degrave, that long-nosed, skinny woman with bad teeth who miraculously inherited two million from the brewer and who has so beautifully put on weight and now laughs with such lovely teeth. That's all there is, my darling . . . And it's time for me to send you, all jumbled together on this line, the longing, the desires, and the soft and ardent and nameless things my heart is filled with, without its emptying no matter how completely I throw them at your adored feet, which I kiss with submission and with faith.

Fradique

XVII

To Eduardo Prado

PARIS, 1888

My dear Prado,

Your excellent letter was received on the holy day of Saint John in this cool refuge of groves and fountains where I am resting up from the somber splendors of Amazonia and the fatigue of the waters of the Atlantic.

I shall not forget the cheese pastries from Sapa. Ficalho, who dined and philosophized here yesterday *sub tegmine fagi*,[31] received from my hands the exact study and the prints of his compatriot on the *Mucuna glabra*. The two vases from the Rato with the Cross of Avis leave tomorrow and may God keep them filled with those *roses of life*, always renewed and fresh, that Anacreon promises the just. All of this was easy and loving work. More difficult and complex is it for me to give you (as you so urgently request) my opinion of your Brazil . . . And you, less skeptical than Pilate, demand the Truth, the naked truth, without chauvinisms or decorations . . . Where do I keep the Truth? It is not, unfortunately, on my Saragoça estate that I have the divine spring where it lives in hiding under the cypress and the laurel. I can only communicate the impression of a man who passed through and saw. And it is my impression that the Brazilians, from the Emperor on down to the worker, are going about undoing and, therefore, ruining Brazil.

At the beginning of the century, some fifty-five years ago, the Brazilians, free of two ills of their youth—gold and the colonial regime—had a unique moment and one of wonderful promise. A people cured, free, strong, in full health once more, with everything to grow in their splendid soil, the Brazilians on that radiant day could found such special civilization as they wished, with the full freedom that an artist has to mold inert clay on his tripod and make of it, according to his will, a jar or a god. I don't mean to be disrespectful, my dear Prado, but I have the impression that Brazil has opted for the jar.

Everything about them, from the sky over them to the natural disposition that governed them, everything patently indicated to the Brazilians that they should be a rural people. Don't be taken aback, my most civilized friend. I don't mean that the Brazilians should continue the patriarchy of Abraham and the Book of Genesis, reproducing Canaan in Minas Gerais and herding cattle about their tents, dressing in hides, and in constant argument with Jehovah. Even less for them to adopt the Arcadian model and for all citizens to be Tithyruses and Marilias, lying under the boughs of a beech and playing the flute, as in the eclogues . . . No. What I meant was for Brazil, unencumbered by its immoral gold and its King John VI, to set itself up on its vast domains and there quietly allow its broad rural life to bring into being, with a vigorous and pure originality, ideas, feelings, customs, literature, art, an ethic, a philosophy, and a whole harmonious civilization of its own, one that is only Brazilian, only from Brazil, and with nothing owed to the books, the styles, or the imported habits of Europe. What I would like (and what would constitute a useful force in the universe) is a Brazil that is natural, spontaneous, and genuine: a national, a Brazilian Brazil, and not the Brazil that I saw, made with old pieces of Europe brought over on steamships and hurriedly assembled, like cheap cloth in the marketplace, in an unrelated natural environment that makes the mold and the stains stand out all the more.

That's what I would like, my esteemed friend! And just think now how delightfully habitable a Brazilian Brazil would be. Rich, vast plantations everywhere. Simple, white-washed houses, beautiful only in the luxury of the space, the air, the water, the shade. Large families where the activities of cultivation, hunting, and vigorous exercise would make people robust and thus perfect their beauty. A frugal and healthy life; clear and simple ideas and a great peacefulness of the soul; no knowledge of false vanities; serious and enduring affections . . .

But, good heavens! Here I am rewriting Book II of the *Georgics! Hanc olim veteres vitam coluere Sabini* . . .[32] That was how the old Sabines lived, idem Romulus and Remus. That was how valiant Etruria grew, that was how ever beautiful Rome, taking in its seven hills, became the marvel of the world. I am not demanding for Brazil the golden and classical virtues of the Age of Saturn. I only would like it to live a simple, strong, and original life like that other half of America, North America, lived before industrialism, mercantilism, capitalism, dollarism, and all those social *-isms* that are undermining it today and making it so tumultuous and crude. That was when the colonists were puritan and grave, when the plow was ennobling, when instruction and education were in the hands of working men, when poets and moralists lived in wooden houses built by their hands, when great doctors covered the land on horseback and carried their medicines unceremoniously in the pouches attached to their saddles, when governors and presidents of the Republic came from humble farms, when the women wove the cloth for their bed linens and the carpets for their homes, when the simplicity of the manners came from the innocence of the hearts, when tillers of the soil formed a class which, by virtue of its knowledge and its intelligence, could fulfill with nobility all the duties of the state, and when the new America startled the whole world with its originality, strong and fruitful.

Well then, my dear friend! Instead of choosing this existence, which would have given Brazil a civilization of its own, one genuine and admired for its solidity and beauty, what did the Brazilians do? No sooner did the ships of King John VI disappear into the Atlantic mists than the Brazilians, masters of Brazil, abandoned the fields and ran to cluster in cities, proceeding to copy messily our European civilization in what there was of the gaudiest and the easiest to copy. In a short time Brazil was covered with alien institutions, almost contrary to its nature and its destiny, hurriedly translated from old French textbooks. Newspapers, editorials, puffed-up constitutional rhetoric, the tyranny of public opinion, impudent polemics, all the intrigues of politicking immediately became common evils.

Old and simple customs were abandoned with disdain. Every man sought a baronet's crown for his head and at 115 degrees in the shade ladies began to perspire inside their grosgrains and thick velvets. In houses now there wasn't a single honest wicker chair where a body could have some rest and coolness at the end of the day, but there was a beginning of bright-colored damasks, furniture with gilded feet, drapes with thick fringes, and all the weight of upholstered decoration with which Paris and London defend themselves from the snow and where microbes triumph. There was the immediate spread of the illnesses of old civilizations: tuberculosis, infections, dyspepsia, neuroses, and a whole silent deterioration of the race. And Brazil was radiant because it was becoming just as rickety as Europe, which has three thousand years of excess and three thousand years of banquets and revolutions behind it!

In the meantime Brazil now possessed democracy, industrialism, a stockholding society in all the delirium of its infinite forms, electric lights, and the "French poison" under the major brands of champagne and the novel. It was ripe for all major refinements and it ordered the arrival, by steamer, of Positivism and comic opera. It was a huge orgy: sabiá birds were taught to warble *Madame Angot* and shopkeepers quoted Auguste Comte . . . Why prolong the painful inventory? Quite soon nothing remained of Brazil, of the generous and old Brazil, not even Brazilians, because there were only doctors and lawyers, which are different entities. The entire nation had become doctorified. From north to south, in all Brazil, there is nothing, I haven't found anything but doctors. Doctors with all manner of insignias, all manner of functions: doctors with a sword and commanding soldiers, doctors with a wallet and founding banks, doctors with depth gauges and captaining ships, doctors with a whistle and directing the police, doctors with a lyre and reciting songs, doctors with a plumb line and constructing buildings, doctors with scales and ministering drugs, doctors

with nothing at all and governing the state. All of them doctors. Dr. Lt. Colonel
. . . Dr. Vice-Admiral . . . Dr. Chief of Police . . . Dr. Architect . . . Intelligent,
educated, polished, and affable men, but all doctors. And the title isn't harmless:
it makes an imprint on one's character. Such a disproportionate legion of doctors
has enwrapped all Brazil in an atmosphere of doctory.

Well, then, the special feature of doctory is to pay no attention to realities
but to conceive of everything *a priori* and try to organize and govern the world
according to the rules in textbooks. Its most complete expression can be found
in that doctor, a minister of the Empire, who in public matters never consulted
the needs of the nation but thumbed anxiously through books to find out what,
in vaguely similar cases, Guizot had done in France or Pitt in England. It is
these doctors, Brazilian in nationality but not in nationalism, who more and
more every day are denationalizing Brazil, killing its native originality with the
doctoral insistence on dressing it, morally and materially, in a European-cut suit
made of Gallicisms with touches of Anglicisms and some vague Germanism.

In that way the free genius of the nation has been constantly falsified,
twisted, and turned away from its original manifestation in everything: in politics by the doctrines of Europe, in literature by the schools of Europe, in society
by the fashions of Europe.

The famous letter of freedom of August 29, 1825, was of no use for the
country's intelligence. Intellectually Brazil is still a colony, a colony of the boulevard. Letters, science, customs, institutions, none of it is national, everything
comes from outside, in crates on steamships from Bordeaux, so that this world,
which proudly calls itself the New World, is, in reality, a very old world, rutted
with wrinkles, those diseased wrinkles that twenty centuries of literature have
given us.

I went all over Brazil in search of the new and all I found was the old, what
has already been old for a hundred years in our Europe: our old ideas, our old
costumes, our old formulas, and all of it older, threadbare, entirely done in from
travel and sunlight. Do you know what it seemed to me like, to sum up my impression in one material image, as Buffon recommends? It was that all through
Brazil an ancient and shabby carpet has been laid out, one made from the cut-
tings of European civilization and covering the natural and fresh carpeting of
the grass and flowers of the soil . . . Can you conceive of a greater horror? Over
a perfumed garden in full bloom, covering everything, smothering everything,
open roses and their buds, a heavy woolen carpet, full of holes and dusty, smelling
of mold!

And is there a cure for such a severe affliction? Of course there is. Pull off the suffocating carpet. But what wise Hercules will undertake this virtuous labor? I don't know.

In any case, I do believe that Brazil still has a chance to reenter a national and completely Brazilian life. When the Empire disappears and in its place comes that Jacobin-Positivist Republic that is already throbbing in the schools and which the doctors of the pen will necessarily make, in partnership with the doctors of the sword; when in turn that Jacobin-Positivist Republic withers, like a plant placed artificially on top of the ground and without roots in it, and disappears completely one morning, carried off by the European and doctoral wind that brought it; and when again, without a struggle and by a simple logical conclusion, there appears in the Paço de São Cristóvão a new emperor or king— Brazil, I repeat, at that moment will have a chance to cast off the "European carpet" that covers it, making it ugly and smothering it. The chance lies in the hope that the new emperor or king is a strong young man, healthy and handsome, quite Brazilian, who loves nature and detests books.

I see no other salvation. But on that happy day when Brazil, with a heroic effort, decides to be Brazilian and part of the *new world*, there will be a great nation in the world. Its men have intelligence, its women have beauty, and both have the most beautiful and best of qualities, kindness. And the nation that has kindness, intelligence, beauty (and coffee, in these sublime proportions) can count on a superb historical future once it convinces itself that it is better to be an original tiller of the soil than a doctor poorly translated from the French.

Do not hold all this disorderly frankness against me and believe me when I say that I am as great a friend of Brazil as I am of you.

Fradique Mendes

XVIII
To Clara . . .
(Transl.)
PARIS, . . .

My friend,

It is true that I am leaving and on a very long and distant journey, which will be like a disappearance. And it is also true that I am undertaking it so brusquely, not because of any curiosity of spirit, for there are no longer any curiosities left, but to put an end in a most worthy and beautiful way to a relationship like ours, which should never be stained by a tormented and slow final agony.

Of course, now that I painfully know that over our so healthy and strong love there will shortly follow the law of universal disappearance and the end of things, I could, we both could try, through a skillful and delicate effort of heart and intelligence, for a fictitious prolongation. But would that attempt be worthy of you, of me, of our loyalty—and of our passion? No! We would only be preparing the way for a wretched torment, without the beauty of the torments that the soul savors and accepts in pure moments of faith, and it would all be tarnished and made ugly by impatience, recriminations, unconfessed repentances, false revivals of desire, and all the enervation of satiety. We would not halt the march of the inexorable law and one day we would face each other as empty, irreparably sad, and filled with bitterness because of that useless struggle. And of a cause so pure, so healthy, and so luminous as was our love all that would be left to us would be, present and pungent, the memory of remnants and rags torn by our hands and dragged along in the final dust of everything.

No! Such an ending would be intolerable. And then, since all struggles are noisy and cannot be controlled or closed up secretly in the heart, we would certainly finally let peep out for the world to see feelings that we were hiding out of pride, not out of caution; and the world would learn of our love precisely when it has already lost the height and grandeur that came close to sanctifying it . . . But in the end, what does the world matter? For us only, who for each other and completely were the whole world, we must avoid the slow, degrading decomposition of our love.

For the perpetual pride of our hearts it is necessary that of this love, which must perish like everything that lives, even the sun, there remain for us a memory so pure and perfect that it alone, all by itself, can give us during the melancholy future a bit of that happiness and enchantment that the love itself gave us when it was in us a sublime reality that governed our very being.

Death that came about in the fullness of a person's beauty and strength was considered by the ancients to be the greatest gift of the gods, especially for those who were left behind, because the beloved face that had passed could remain forever in their memory with its natural vigor and healthy beauty, and not emaciated and deteriorated by fatigue, tears, despair, and pain. That is how our love should remain, too.

Therefore, as soon as I caught its first drooping and desolately verified that time had touched it with the coldness of its scythe, I decided to leave, to disappear. Our love, my dear friend, will in that way be like a miraculous flower that grew, bloomed, gave all its aroma and, never cut, never shaken by the wind or the rain, nor the least bit withered, remains on its solitary stem, still enchanting our eyes with its colors when they turn to it from a distance, and through the ages perfumes our lives forever.

Of my life I know, at least, that it will be perpetually illuminated and perfumed by its memory. I am, in truth, like one of those shepherds who in olden times, strolling pensively on a hilltop in Greece, suddenly saw, before their ecstatic eyes, Venus magnificent and loving as she opened her white arms to them. For a moment the mortal shepherd rested his head on the divine breast and heard the murmur of a divine sigh. Then there was a slight tremor and he would find himself before a retreating cloud that was rising up and disappearing into the air in the midst of a bright flight of doves. Thereupon he would pick up his crook and go back down the hill . . . But forever, all through his life, he preserved an ineffable captivation. The years would roll by, his stock might die or the wind carry off the roof of his hut, and all the miseries of old age would fall upon him—but his soul would glow in splendor and a feeling of ultra-human glory lifted him up above the transitory and the perishable, for on that fresh May morning, over on top of the hill, he had had his moment of becoming divine amidst the thyme and the myrtle.

Farewell, my friend. For the incomparable happiness that you have given me may you be perpetually blessed.

Eça de Queirós (for Fradique)

Notes

by Anna M. Klobucka

[1] *La Légende des siècles* (*The Legend of the Centuries*) is a collection of poems by Victor Hugo, published in three series between 1859 and 1883; Hugo lived on the island of Guernsey, off the coast of Normandy, from 1855 to 1873. The Cenacle (Port. Cenáculo) was an informal discussion group composed of some of the leading late nineteenth-century Portuguese intellectuals, including Eça de Queirós.

[2] "And yet you will be like this excrement, / This horrible stench, / O star of my eyes, sun of my being, / You, my angel, my passion." Trans. Geoffrey Wagner, in *Selected Poems of Charles Baudelaire* (New York: Grove Press, 1974).

[3] "Then, my beauty, say to the vermin / Which will eat you with kisses, / That I have kept the shape and the divine substance / Of my decomposed loves!" Trans. Wagner, *Selected Poems*.

[4] "Look at something new."

[5] "Thanks be to you, my blessed St. John, for I have seen something new!"

[6] "Betrothment of the Tomb" (Port. "O Noivado do Sepulcro") was a Romantic poem by Soares de Passos (1826–60), published in 1856. The author of the poem "Ave Caesar" was José da Silva Mendes Leal (1818–86).

[7] A reference to the French writer François-René de Chateaubriand (1768–1848) and his novella *René* (1802).

[8] *Contemporary Portugal* (*Portugal Contemporâneo*) is a book by Oliveira Martins (1845–94) published in 1881.

[9] *The Death of Don Juan* (*A Morte de D. João*) and *The Muse on Vacation* (Port. *A Musa em Férias*) are works by Guerra Junqueiro (1850–1923) published, respectively, in 1874 and 1879.

[10] Reference to Antero de Quental (1842–91), whose volume of *Modern Odes* (*Odes Modernas*) was published in 1865.

[11] Counselor Acácio (Conselheiro Acácio) is a character in Eça de Queirós's novel *O Primo Basílio* (1878).

[12] "Sir, you are observing us too closely for your judgment not to be biased; I invite you, therefore, in your best interest, and so that you may obtain a more accurate overview of Russia, to go watch it from further away, in your beautiful house in Paris!"

[13] "Sir, I received your invitation, which contains a lot of intolerance and three errors in French."

[14] "Fradique's thaw."

[15] "Unexpected and sudden."

[16] "Always lucky, this Fradique!"

[17] "By right of beauty and wisdom."

[18] "Through earth to heaven."

[19] "He who lives unnoticed lives well."

[20] "It is his genius that effervesces."

[21] "It thinks, therefore it is."

[22] "Now and forever."

[23] "To see this great Ortigan!"

[24] "A large and beautiful woman."

[25] "Ah yes, it is so good to unwind!"

[26] "At your disposal."

[27] "With what songs to sing [about] you, wine from Raetia?"

[28] "God has given us this tranquility in the shadows of most beautiful Portugal."

[29] "I love, therefore I am."

[30] "For all the time to come."

[31] "In the shade of a leafy beech" (from the first line of Virgil's *Eclogue I*).

[32] "Long ago the old Sabines lived this life."